When the Streets Clap Back 2

Lock Down Publications and Ca$h
Presents
When the Streets Clap Back 2
A Novel by *Jibril Williams*

WHEN THE STREETS CLAP BACK 2
Lock Down Publications
P.O. Box 870494
Mesquite, Tx 75187

Visit our website at
www.lockdownpublications.com

Copyright 2018 When the Streets Clap Back 2

Lock Down Publications
Like our page on Facebook: Lock Down Publications @
www.facebook.com/lockdownpublications.ldp
Cover design and layout by: **Dynasty Cover Me**
Book interior design by: **Shawn Walker**
Edited by: **Tisha Andrews**

Stay Connected with Us!

Text **LOCKDOWN** to 22828 to stay up-to-date with new releases, sneak peaks, contests and more...
Or CLICK HERE to sign up.

Thank you!

Like our page on Facebook:

Lock Down Publications: Facebook

Join Lock Down Publications/The New Era Reading Group

Follow us on Instagram:

Lock Down Publications: Instagram

Email Us: We want to hear from you!

WHEN THE STREETS CLAP BACK 2
Submission Guideline.

Submit the first three chapters of your completed manuscript to ldpsubmissions@gmail.com, subject line: Your book's title. The manuscript must be in a .doc file and sent as an attachment. Document should be in Times New Roman, double spaced and in size 12 font. Also, provide your synopsis and full contact information. If sending multiple submissions, they must each be in a separate email.

Have a story but no way to send it electronically? You can still submit to LDP/Ca$h Presents. Send in the first three chapters, written or typed, of your completed manuscript to:

LDP: Submissions Dept
Po Box 870494
Mesquite, Tx 75187

DO NOT send original manuscript. Must be a duplicate.

Provide your synopsis and a cover letter containing your full contact information.

Thanks for considering LDP and Ca$h Presents.

.

Chapter 1

40 fought back tears as he stared down at his childhood friend Skalez lying in his casket. He flexed his jaw muscles and his nostrils flared up as pure rage boiled inside him.

"Fam," 40's voice cracked as he whispered to Skalez. "Who the fuck did this shit to you? How you get caught slipping?" Finally, he couldn't fight his tears any longer and the tears began to fall freely. "Block gone, now you. Who is going to hold me down, huh?" he asked, getting a little too loud. "Fam, I'm going to make the streets bleed about this one." He wiped the snot from his running nose with the back of his hand. With her arm entwined with his, Paula rested her head on shoulder.

"He looks so handsome," Paula spoke, not looking at 40 but at Skalez. 40 didn't reply. He just patted Paula's arm to comfort her.

The funeral home had done a great job with Skalez. He had eight, neatly braided cornrows in his head. The custom made Gucci suit he was draped in gave the true meaning to the statement casket sharp. The black casket trimmed in gold showed that he was a boss of his time and in his own lane. Finally, Paula lifted her head off 40's shoulder.

"Come on, 40. Other people want to see him and pay their last respects," Paula stated, wiping her eyes and giving his arm a slight tug. 40 looked over his shoulder at the people standing behind him waiting to view Skalez's body. He was reluctant to move, but he let Paula escort him to the first row of pews facing Skalez's casket.

Paula locked fingers with 40 when she took her seat next to him. He felt a little uncomfortable with Paula's sudden affection, but he chalked it up as emotional stress related to loosing someone. 40 watched everyone like a hawk who came to send his comrade off. Being a street nigga, he knew that sometimes the answer you were looking for was in their body language. Not what a nigga discloses out his mouth.

Guilt started to ride 40's conscious. He was thinking if he would have listened to Skalez and got out the game, he would've been there to watch homie's back instead of being in jail. They had done so much grimy shit together to niggas that Skalez's killers could be anybody in that room or the same people that killed Block. He was wrecking his brain trying to figure out who was behind Skalez's death, but his instincts told him his death had something to do with Lance.

At the thought of Lance, 40 saw a familiar face. It had been a minute since he saw the young nigga Lil BJ. In fact, he hadn't since they pulled that caper on Lance. Him and Lil BJ made eye contact with one another before he made his way over to him.

"Fam, I'm truly sorry for your loss," he expressed to 40, extending his hand. He nodded, accepting his hand.

"This here is Skalez's wifey, Paula," 40 told him, pointing to Paula who sat next to him.

"My deepest sympathy go out to you, Paula," Lil BJ replied, acknowledging her as he paid his respects.

"Yo, Lil BJ. I'm gon' to need to holla at you, so let's exchange numbers before you leave." He almost wanted to ask 40 what he needed to speak to him about, but he didn't.

"A'ight. That's cool, fam. Oh, welcome back," he said, walking away.

40 stared at Lil BJ's back. He sensed he had a different demeanor about himself since the last time he saw him. He was thinking maybe he could use him on his team to find out who had killed Skalez.

It seemed like the whole city came out to send him off, but 40 knew half of the people that showed up were really there to confirm his death.

"Oh Lord, my baby!" Skalez's mother, Mona, yelled out, falling to her knees in front of her son's casket. The outburst sent everyone into tears. Paula rushed to Mona's side to console her. 40 couldn't take it anymore before the tears started back flowing again as he made his exit. He needed some air. He walked out the funeral home, pulling a pack of Newport 100's out his black Gucci slacks' pocket. He lit a cigarette and inhaled deeply. He watched a woman standing a few feet in front of him. Releasing the nicotine from his lungs, 40 spoke.

"There's only one ass like that in the whole city of Newport News. What's good, Tashia?"

Tashia was about to catch a straight attitude, but after hearing her name, she turned around to see 40 standing behind her. She rushed to him, hugging him tightly.

"When the fuck did you get out? They killed him, 40. They killed Skalez." Tashia started crying as 40 hugged her just as tightly.

"I know. I'm going to find out who did this," he replied, rocking her back and forth in his arms.

"I see we all doing the group hug thing," Wallo said, walking up and bear hugging the both of them. "I guess it's just us, right?" Neither 40 nor Tashia answered. "I'm not gon' let this ride," Wallo spoke through clenched teeth.

"Me either," 40 and Tashia spoke at the same time.

JIBRIL WILLIAMS

Chapter 2

Tashia got out of bed and stretched out her tense body. Being at the funeral yesterday and seeing Skalez was stressful. Looking at the clock that rested on her nightstand next to her bed, she realized she had over-slept. It was 11:50. She had told 40 and Wallo to come over at noon.

Walking into the bathroom and copping a squat on the toilet, Tashia relieved her bladder. It seemed she had to piss for five minutes straight. She wiped herself good and washed her hands. Then she squeezed some Colgate on her toothbrush and began to bush her teeth.

Knock, knock, knock.

The rapid knocks on Tashia's door interrupted her morning brush. She made her way to the front door, still brushing her teeth. Looking through the peephole, she stared at 40.

Opening the door, she waved him in and threw up one finger telling him to wait one minute. She turned and walked away, giving 40 a good view of her backside. Her 43-inch ass ate up her boy shorts like a Cambodian refugee. Seeing her like that with nothing on but a t-shirt and boy shorts reminded 40 of a song by Adina Howard called "T-Shirt & Panties".

40 realized he'd been home for eight days and still hadn't got his dick wet. Tashia was a perfect candidate for him. She had that Buffy "Da Body" body, standing a perfect 5'10" and weighing 156 pounds with super thick thighs and double D breast. Tashia was a straight stack house. Her pretty face with cocoa brown skin was im-peccable. You couldn't even tell that she had given birth to two children.

40's dick stood rock hard in his Polo jeans. When Tashia came back in the living room wearing a pair of

Prada sweat pants, he eyeballed her with admiration. Tashia being a person that didn't miss much, caught him looking.

"What the fuck got you looking at me all goo-goo eyed?" she asked with a smirk on her face.

"You know I've been home eight days. With all the shit going on with Skalez getting killed, I haven't had a chance to get some pussy yet." 40 stood smiling, clutching his dick through his jeans. He gave Tashia that look that said "what's up".

"Oh yeah?" she replied seductively, walking over to 40 and invading his personal space. "Let me see it," Tashia said, extending her hand with an opened palm. 40 wasted no time unbuckling his jeans and placing his 9-inch manhood in her hand. She squeezed it, making eye contact with him. She could feel his dick thumping in her hand beating like a heartbeat. "Damn, 40. Nice."

Tashia slightly stroked his manhood. "You nice and thick just like I like it." Pre-cum began to ooze from 40's bell pepper-shaped head.

Tashia took her thumb, making small circles around the head of his dick using his pre-cum to lubricate it.

She untied her sweat pants, letting them drop to the floor and pulling her lime green boy shorts down along with them. Then she bent over the arm of the couch and arched her back, making her fat ass spread wide open. 40 ran his hand between her legs, touching the pussy to check for wetness. He brought his fingers back out saturated in her juices.

"Come on, 40. Don't play with it! Fuck it!" Tashia demanded as she moaned.

40 entered her from the back. Her pussy was warm like an oven, hugging his dick like a pair of small gloves. "Damn! Fuck, Tashia!" he belted, slow stroking and pushing into her deeper.

Boom! Boom! Boom!

They both jumped, hearing knocks at the door. 40 snatched his dick out and pulled his pants up. Tashia did the same.

"Who the fuck is that?" 40 asked, snatching the compact 9-millimeter from out of his back pocket.

"I don't know," Tashia replied, making her way to the door. 40 stood right behind her, clutching his 9-millimeter.

"Who is it?" she asked through the door.

"It's Wallo."

"Damn, I forgot he was coming," she told him, unlocking the door to let him in. 40 went and took a seat on the couch. He was mad as hell Wallo interrupted his piece of ass.

"What's up, fam," Wallo said, entering the house and giving him some dap.

"Ain't nothing, Wallo. Have you heard anything in the street about Skalez's death?" he asked him, getting straight to the point.

"Fam, I haven't heard shit," he replied, firing the blunt up that rested behind his ear. "All I know is my cousin is dead." Tashia sat down in her love seat across from 40, tucking one leg underneath her. "But I tell you what though, fam," Wallo said as he inhaled the blunt, letting the smoke seep through his nose. "If we find out who Skalez bodied before he died, that would lead us to who else was involved," he said, passing the blunt to 40.

40 respected how Wallo's mind was working.

"That shouldn't be hard since Skalez dropped dude in his own house. All I got to do is get with Paula and ask her. If she don't know, I'll have her contact the detective that's investigating his death. They should be able to tell her the name of the other deceased person," 40 told him in between hitting the blunt.

"I'm not going to lie. Y'all, I think this have some-thing to do with Lance," Tashia said, making eye contact with 40.

"I've been having the same feeling Tashia, but I just can't make the connection," 40 admitted.

"Hold the fuck up! Who the fuck is Lance?" Wallo asked, sitting next to Tashia on the love seat.

"Lance is some nigga we jacked from New York. Remember that night we had Tashia go to you and grab that counting machine from you?" 40 asked.

"Yeah, fam. I remember. That was the night Skalez called a nigga early in the morning about that." Wallo stroked his beard as he talked.

"Well, that's the night we hit Lance and that's the night Skalez retired from the game."

"So, you both think this has something to do with the nigga Lance?" Wallo asked.

They both nodded their heads in agreement.

"I just find that hard to believe because Block was straight up killed. Nothing was even taken from him. But my cousin was robbed for everything and killed. Even after he killed the one who tried to rob him," he replied, getting up and grabbing the blunt out of 40's hand.

"Well, I think you and 40 should go holla at Paula and see what you can find out from her. Let's start there," Tashia said, rubbing her fingertips into her temple in a circular motion trying to relieve the stress she felt.

"A'ight, I'm gon' head out and see what I can find out from Paula. I'll get with both of you when I got something." 40 got up and headed to the door, leaving Tashia behind with a wet pussy. She wished he would've stayed to finish what they started.

"I'm gone too, Tashia," Wallo said, getting up to leave with him.

Chapter 3

Lil BJ looked at his bed covered with money. His mind was drunk on how much money he'd just counted. "Damn, that nigga Skalez was loaded," he said to himself, walking away with $329,000. He had never in his life seen that much money at one time. Truth be told, he'd never even had $10,000 at one time.

The night after the caper, Lil BJ had trouble sleeping. He kept thinking the police or somebody that fucked with Skalez would run up in his house and kill him. He stayed in his room for two days with his gun in his hand watching his bedroom door. The second day, his sister Vanessa started banging on his bedroom door with the news that Lil Chris had been killed in a home invasion.

He had to think fast as he grabbed $10,000 from the money he had took from Skalez, heading to Lil Chris's mother's house. He gave the money to her to bury Chris with no problems. He told her they hustled and saved money together, but he wanted her to send his little homie off in style. Instead, his mother thought otherwise, cremating him for $2,000 and pocketing the rest.

Lil BJ knew with this type of money, he had to move like a grown man. There was no room for any wrong moves. He knew with one misstep, the streets would attack him like a pack of wolves. Plus, he knew niggas in the streets would not allow Skalez's murderer ride.

He loaded the money back into the Nike gym bag, putting $30,000 to the side. He grabbed the diamond-crusted Jesus piece chain off the bed, holding it high in the air. He took the chain off Lil Chris's dead body the night he got killed.

"Damn, Chris. This is all I got left of you," he said to the Jesus piece as if it was Lil Chris himself. He placed the chain in the Nike bag with the rest of the money, putting the bag in the back of his closet. "Yo, Ma! Aye, Vanessa! Let me holla at y'all in the kitchen," he yelled through the house.

"Boy, what in the hell you want and why are you doing all that damn yelling?" his mother asked, coming out her bedroom with a lighter and stem in her hand.

"Ma, just sit down. I need to talk to you about something important," he told her, leaning against the kitchen sink.

"What, Lil BJ?" Vanessa shot back, coming into the kitchen with her usual attitude.

"Just sit the fuck down and hear me out." Vanessa took a seat next to her mother at the kitchen table.

He looked at both women. He knew these two people were his real family and he loved them. "Some things around here are about to change. I don't know if you both have noticed or not—" he started then paused, trying to find the right words. "But when these changes come full circle, I need to make sure you two are out of the way. Vanessa, I know we fight like cats and dogs, but that shit stops today. From now on, it's all loyalty and no hate. And Ma, I need you to get clean, but only if you want to. You a grown ass woman and I can't make you do nothing you don't want to do. But know as your son, I need you and I need you clean," he said with sincerity.

He then pulled the thirty stacks out his pocket. "Vanessa, I need you to find a nice place in a nice neighborhood for you and Ma. I don't care if it's all the way in Hampton. I just need it done in the next five days. Don't worry about taking anything with you. We're buying all new shit." He handed his sister $30,000. Vanessa and his mother both started crying.

"Where you get all this money from?" Vanessa asked through tears.

"Don't worry about all that. Please, just do what I asked you to do. I need both of you out this house tonight. Go to a hotel until you find a place to stay."

His mother was shocked to see her son becoming the man of the house. She knew she wasn't strong enough to get clean, but she decided to give it her best shot. "What are we going to do about this house?" she asked, while wiping her eyes.

"I got other plans for it, Ma. Just help Vanessa and I'll take care of everything else," he instructed her, walking over to kiss them both on their foreheads. "Now, I need both of you gone in two hours," he said before he walked out the front door.

JIBRIL WILLIAMS

Chapter 4

"Hello," Paula answered her phone in a sleepy voice.

"What's up, Paula? How you holding up?" 40 asked.

"Oh, hi 40. I'm making it the best way I know how. That's taking it one day at a time."

"That's all we can do, Paula. Take it one day at a time. Hey, are you sleep or something?" he asked.

"No, I'm not sleep. I was just taking a nap, but I got to get up and feed the baby," Paula replied, getting up off the couch. She shook the numbness in her arm from sleeping on it.

"Okay, that's cool. Look, Paula. I'm not too far from your house. I need to swing by there and holla at you about something." 40 checked his rearview mirror before switching lanes.

"Alright, perfect timing for me because I have a few things I need to talk to you about, too. How long before you get here?" she asked, walking into the kitchen to grab a bottle of milk out the refrigerator.

"I'll be there in about 20 minutes."

Paula was gorgeous standing at 5'4", her golden skin highlighted by her honey-brown eyes and natural black mane that ran down her back putting a Brazilian hair-weave to shame. Even after she gave birth to her daughter Akeemah a few months earlier, she still maintained her perky C-cups and 40-inch ass. Paula placed the bottle in a pot of water on the stove to warm up her daughter's milk.

She went to check on her daughter who was still resting in her bed. She then made her way to the bathroom to wash her face. Catching a glimpse of herself in the mirror, she stopped to get a better look at the woman she saw. The person that stared back at her was like a stranger, one that seemed to be missing something.

Paula knew what she was missing. It was her better half, her friend, her lover, her life partner. She was missing Skalez. She closed her eyes, remembering the first time they met. She was leaving her dorm at NSU.

"Girl, are you going to Arts lecture today?" Paula asked her dorm mate Shay.

"Yeah, girl. I'm going. I can't afford to miss too many more of them classes," Shay replied, rolling her eyes at the thought of going to that boring class. "Paula, we need to get us a car so we don't have to walk to campus," Shay complained about the 2-block walk to campus.

"Come on now. You know we can't afford a car on our budget. Plus, the campus is only two blocks from here. Sheesh! Girl, you are lazy!" Paula said, giving Shay a hard time. They heard a horn that caught their attention.

Beep! Beep! Beep!

"Hey, beautiful!" the driver of the white Dodge Durango shouted out his window.

"Hey!" Shay responded.

"You beautiful too, but I'm talking to your friend," the driver stated, cruising beside them in his truck.

Paula heard the man, only giving him a quick wiggle of her fingers, acknowledging his presence as she kept it moving. The driver wasn't too pleased with the response he'd gotten, so he doubled park, hit his hazard lights and got out.

"Damn, you always get all the good ones, Paula. Look at him. He's handsome as fuck," Shay whispered to her friend, while bumping her with her elbow trying get her to look. Paula cut her eyes at the approaching guy, admiring his swag and name brand labels.

"Excuse me, Miss! Excuse me!"

"I'm 'Miss' now, but a few minutes ago, I was 'Hey beautiful'. So, which one is it? You making a sister feel old with all that Miss stuff," Paula said with a slight attitude, playing hard to get.

"I'm sorry about all that, shawty. But when I saw you, I was so deeply overwhelmed by your beauty, I had to yell to get your attention. Me, after seeing you, had to know your name. I swear if God created anything more beautiful than you, he must have kept it for himself," Skalez said with sincerity and confidence.

Shay's mouth dropped at the smoothness of this stranger's lines. Her heart was fluttering. No one had ever approached her in the manner he just did. She really didn't know what to say, blushing as they made eye contact.

"So, are you going to tell me your name?" the slick talking strange asked, breaking her eye contact.

"Oh, yeah," Paula replied, giggling. *"It's Paula."*

"Nice to meet you, Paula. My name is Jermaine, but you can call me Skalez."

"Skalez? Like scales on a fish?" Shay asked, interrupting Skalez and Paula's connection.

"Naw, baby. Like the scales you weigh stuff on. But I spell it S-K-A-L-E-Z," he said, correcting her friend.

"Well, I like your government name better, so I'll call you that."

***

The ringing of Paula's phone brought her back from her trip down memory lane.

"Hello," she said, answering the phone as she walked out the bathroom to check on the bottle.

"Paula, it's 40. I'm walking up to the house. Open the door."

She hung up and opened the door. "Hi, 40. What's up?" she said, giving up a weak smile. 40 could see the hurt and sadness in her eyes.

"Ain't too much going on. I just came over to check up on you and Akeemah." 40 walked in the condo, closing the door behind him. "Damn, Paula. You moving or something?" he inquired, seeing all the boxes covering the living room floor.

"I'm moving to DC with my grandmother. I got to get out of Bad News, Newport News." Paula let out a sigh. "There's nothing else here for me," she told him as her eyes began to water.

"What you mean there's nothing else here?" 40 asked, walking over to her and placing both of his hands on her shoulders. "What about Skalez's mom, Mona? What about me, Paula? I loved Skalez just like he was my own flesh and blood." 40 dug his fingertips into Paula's shoulders, getting loud. "You got the businesses here, Fresh To Death Cuts and Heavenly Fashion Beauty and Nail salon." 40 looked into Paula's eyes.

"No, I don't. When Skalez died, I lost everything! When he died, I lost the best part of me! My daughter will never know her father!" Paula put her head down and started crying. "I got to get out this place 40. This whole city reminds me of Skalez. I'm selling both shops and starting a new life in D.C.," Paula said, wiping her eyes, as she pulled away from him.

The realization of Skalez being robbed and murdered enraged 40, but he held his composure. "Listen, Paula. I need to ask you a question." 40 paused, gathering his thoughts. "The nigga that was found dead in the house with Skalez, who was he? Did the police ever identify him?"

"No!" Paula said with her fists balled up. "It stops here! No more violence! Let Skalez rest! Let it go!" Paula pleaded.

"Let it go! I won't let shit go until every muthafucka that had something to do with his death gets a head up fade with him, whether he's in heaven on hell," 40 yelled, waking Akeemah up who was in the other room.

"40, if that's the case, I can't help you. Please leave." Paula walked to the door and held it opened for him.

40 stopped in front of her with nostrils flaring just staring at her. She refused to make eye contact with him. "What you want for the shops?"

Not looking at him, she mumbled, "One hundred and fifty thousand."

"I'll get that to you as soon as possible. I'm not letting you sale my nigga shit to anybody. You don't even know what he went through to get them shops," 40 said, brushing past Paula.

JIBRIL WILLIAMS

Chapter 5

Lil BJ was running himself raggedy now that his old house became a full-time trap house. He'd been doing all the work by himself since Lil Chris died, not having time to recruit a team. He was too focus on trying to make $5000 day.

His whole perspective of the game had changed over a short period of time. There was no more hustling just to get by. Now, it was hustling to maintain what he had. He'd came across something he'd never experienced in his life and that was power. People saw how he dressed and the cars he started to drive. Even their respect for him began to change, including his mother and sister.

He walked out of his trap house and made his way to his gold Lexus 400 squatting on Ashanti rims. He stood 5' 7", weighing 157 pounds. His swag was on point, wearing a white T-shirt, a pair of Red Monkey Jeans and a pair of brown Tims.

The Polo jacket he wore fitted him to a T and the way he wore his Polo frames made him look a lot older than he really was. His light skin glowed in the fall season. He could tell that it was going to be a cold winter. He pulled his beanie over his left ear as he reached his car and opened the door. He threw the Popeye's chicken bag he had with him in the back seat.

He started up the car and checked his mirrors before pulling away from the curb. Lil BJ's sister put the Lexus in her name for him after they found it at an auction. The police had confiscated it from the last owner, finding drugs in it. He pulled his phone off his hip and dialed a number. It rang twice before someone answered.

"What's up, fam," Bugg said.

"Aye, fam. I'm on 24th street right now. I need you to meet me on Madison," he told him, checking his mirrors for the third time since he turned on 24th street.

"I'm headed your way. I'm on 36th street." Bugg then disconnected the call.

Lil BJ turned the corner on Madison and cruised to the end of the block, deciding to park on the corner across the street from the liquor store. He felt if something went wrong, parking there would allow for a quick get away. He pulled his 9-millimeter from under the seat, checking the chamber to make sure one was in the head. Then he placed the gun in between his legs.

They had developed a good bond over the last few months, but in this game he knew that he couldn't fully trust Bugg. His phone rang and he picked up on the first ring.

"Aye."

"I'm turning on Madison now," Bugg told him.

"Keep straight down to the end of the block. I'm in the gold Lexus," he advised him, hitting the end button on his phone. He watched Bugg drive towards him in his side view mirror. He parked four cars behind him, getting out of his F150, carrying a Footlocker bag.

Bugg walked past Lil BJ's car, stood on the corner and looked around. To the average person, it looked like he was waiting to cross the street to go to the liquor store. But to Lil BJ, he knew he was checking out his surroundings. Bugg turned around and walked back to where he was waiting in his Lexus.

"What's up, fam?" Bugg said as he closed the car door behind him.

"Just cooling, fam. Just them two and half. Where's it at?" Lil BJ asked, watching his mirrors.

"I got them right here, but you know you fucked up, right?"

"Why's that?" he asked, placing his hand in between his legs on his 9-millimeter.

"Man, you stressed to me that I need to stop talking reckless on the phone and I took your advice. Then you show up to buy two and half bricks in a Lexus. Where's the Honda at?" Bugg asked.

"Damn, fam. I'm slipping. My sister got the Honda, but you're right. Thanks for pulling my coat," Lil BJ replied. Bugg just shook his head and passed him the Footlocker bag. Lil BJ took a peek at two and half bricks staring back at him.

"The money is on the backseat in the Popeye's bag," he told him, closing the bag up. Bugg reached in the back seat to get it. He opened it up and grabbed a stack of bills, flipping through them.

"A'ight, fam. I'm out. Hit me when you ready to re-up. I must confess I'm feeling how you're moving. If you keep moving the way you are, you and me can run this city in no time," Bugg said, grabbing the handle.

Tap! Tap! Tap!

They jumped from the tap on the window. Standing on the outside looking in was a face both hadn't seen in a few years. "Bugg, I thought that was your ass, boy. Let a nigga holla at you for a minute."

"Damn, Homicide Jack. You scared the fuck out of me," he said, hesitating to get out the car. Homicide Jack pulled on the door handle, trying to open the side he was sitting on, but the door was locked.

"Hold up, fam," Bugg yelled through the window. Homicide Jack looked around to see if anyone was watching.

"Man, I've been home two months and I'm down on my luck. All I wanted is hold a few dollars," he told him, but he had other plans, trying to shield the handle of his gun that was sticking out his pocket.

"Man, he's going to rob us. Pull off," Bugg told Lil BJ out the corner of his mouth, but he did the opposite as he got out the car leaving his 9-millimeter on the seat.

"What's up, fam. You don't know me, but my name is Lil BJ. I heard so much about you." BJ stepped around the car. Homicide Jack eased his hand on his gun. "I respect OG's and the work they have to put in. You just said you just came home and you're down on your luck. Well here," BJ said, pulling a knot of money out of his pocket. He counted twenty one-hundred dollar bills off the knot and passed it to him. The gesture threw Homicide Jack off his game.

"What's this for?" he questioned.

"For you being you. You don't owe me shit. I just ask that you take the money, and do what you need to do with it. But make sure you buy a phone, then meet me on the corner of twenty-fourth street tomorrow morning eight-thirty if you want to make some money. Just know there's more where that came from," he said, pointing to the bills in Homicide Jack's hand. He smiled and backed away. Lil BJ hit the car window, telling Bugg to get his scary ass out his car.

"Man, fuck you! I'm not scared. He just caught me off guard," Bugg complained.

"Yeah, whatever, nigga." Lil BJ hopped in the Lexus and pushed out. He then dropped the work off to his sister Vanessa and her friend Trici whose job it was to break it down for profit.

Chapter 6

"Oh yes, Toflon. Yes, beat this pussy!" Trici cried out in pleasure, encouraging him to blow her back out. Toflon had her legs draped over his shoulders with a yard of dick in her wet box. "Whose dick is this?" Trici asked in between his strokes.

"It's all yours, ma," Toflon yelled as he felt his nuts draw up, his eruption only moments away. "I'm about to cum, Trici." Toflon started hammering her baby oil slippery pussy.

"Cum in my mouth, baby. I want to taste you," Trici said, while watching Toflon's black pole hammer in and out of her. Hearing she wanted him to cum in her mouth brought Toflon over the top.

"I'm cumming," he growled, quickly pulling out of her. He watched how fast she jumped dead on his dick mouth first, catching his load. She sucked and jerked him off until he was completely empty.

Toflon watched in amazement thinking to himself, *This bitch a vicious dick eater.* "Damn, baby. That was the truth," he said, complimenting her on her dick sucking skills as he pulled his dick out of her mouth.

"Boo, you haven't seen nothing yet," she stated, getting on her knees to kiss him. He turned his head instead, letting the kiss land on his cheek.

Trici was 24-years-old. She was one of them short and shapely, chubby chicks that every hood had. She was cute with her short bob cut that she rocked all the time. She had a set of beautiful eyes that men and women found attractive. Even though her breast weren't big, she made up for it in the ass and hip department. In reality, if she watched what she ate, Trici would he a bad muthafucka.

Trici and Toflon met a few months earlier when she was walking out of Heavenly Fashion Beauty and Nail salon. She'd just gotten after her nails done when Toflon was exiting Fresh to Death Cuts after getting a touch up. He saw her huge ass threatening to bust the seams of her blue jeans she wore. But what really made him really approach her was that "come fuck me walk" she had perfected every since she was a teenager.

Every since then, they had been hooking up every few days to get their freak on. Trici was out to make him hers, falling in love with him. She was willing to do whatever she had to do just to be in his life.

Toflon was smooth to the core his cocoa butter complexion was impeccable. The only mark he had on his body was the word *Conquer* that was scrawled across his back in tattoo ink. Standing five feet eleven inches tall, his lanky frame carried his one hundred and sixty-five pounds effortlessly. He rocked a Caesar cut with a three inch part on the left side of his head. Toflon wore always wore a light smile that exposed the gap between his two front teeth.

Although Trici was sprung on him, he wasn't too quick to fall for her But every time he was around her, she dug her hooks into him just a little deeper. Trici wasn't his ideal top bitch, but she was cute and the pussy and head was straight fire, so he stayed around. Toflon had a three-man stick up team. They were making a name for themselves, but they couldn't find the right lick to set them straight.

Toflon got out the bed and began to put his clothes on. "What's up with that situation you was telling me about, Trici?" he asked.

"I'm still trying to figure some shit out," she replied, laying on her back with her legs wide open. She was trying to entice him to come back to bed to get another round of her goodies.

Toflon, not feeding into her sexual advances, slid his feet into his black Air Force Ones and threw his North Face jacket on. "Well, when you do figure it out, holla at me ASAP. Until then, I got moves to make," he said, walking over and placing two fingers in her pussy as he kissed her on the forehead.

"Mmmm, Toflon," she moaned when his fingers found her G-Spot.

"Keep it wet, baby. I'll be back later." He walked out the bedroom leaving her staring at his back lustfully.

***

"Man, are you sure this nigga sitting on that much dough?" 40 asked Wallo who was sitting behind the wheel of a stolen beat up Ford pickup.

"Fam, be easy. Shit air-tight," Wallo confirmed as he scoped out their intended victim's house.

"What's taking the bitch so long? I thought you said she gets home around nine o'clock? Shit, it's a quarter after nine," 40 complained.

"Shawty must have stopped off somewhere," Wallo replied, not looking at 40. He kept watching the street and the house they were planned to rob as they waited.

"Who you say these niggas are?" 40 questioned him.

"Damn, if I would've known you'd be asking me all these damn questions, I would've never brought your scary ass with me." Wallo gave 40 a sideways glance, aggravated with his steady probing.

"Wallo, you got me fucked up," he told him, getting mad as he tested his gangsta.

He was down with the move, but he wasn't too happy making the move with Wallo. They've never done a caper together. This was Skalez's cousin and on that strength alone, 40 was willing to entertain the caper. Plus, he wanted to make some bread to pay Paula for the

31

shops. There was no way that he was going to let her sell Skalez's shit.

"Showtime, Playboy!" Wallo said, grabbing the Tech 22 off his lap and easing out the truck.

40 followed Wallo's lead, clutching his Glock 19. They caught a beautiful skinny chick getting out her car. Before she even knew what was happening, Wallo had the Tech 22 in her face.

"Bitch, you better not scream," he warned her from behind his mask. The skinny girl was so scared, she pissed on herself right there, souring the nursing scrubs she wore. 40's head was on a swirl, watching for anything that looked out of place.

"Come on. Lets go in the house," Wallo ordered the girl. 40 was behind him, bringing up the rear.

Once inside, they could hear the T.V. playing in the living room. Following closely behind, they caught a brown-skinned dude off guard on the couch watching a re-run of *The Godfather* while drinking a beer. After seeing the two masked men enter the room, his eyes damn near popped out his head.

"Lay your bitch ass on the floor," Wallo demanded, pushing the girl on the floor.

The dude wasted no time getting on the floor. Neither Wallo nor 40 had ever saw the dude before. 40 started going through his pockets making sure that he wasn't strapped.

"Where Man-Man at?" Wallo asked, while 40 searched him.

"He's in the kitchen," his homeboy answered without hesitation.

Wallo then walked over to the girl. "Call Man-Man in here."

"But that's my baby father," she cried.

"Bitch, do you want to die?" he asked her, pressing his gun to the back of her head. The girl shook her head and mouth before she responded.

"No."

"Well, then call his ass." The girl swallowed hard and called out to her baby father.

"Man-Man, can you please come in here?"

A few seconds later, Man-Man came walking out the kitchen holding a ham and cheese sandwich in his hand.

"It's about time you got your ass hom—" he got out his mouth before he was struck in the jaw, bringing him to his knees.

The skinny chick yelled out, "Nooooo!"

"Bitch nigga, where that shit at?" Wallo asked, kicking Man-Man in the side. He fought to stay focused, trying to recover from the blow to his jaw. Man-Man then looked up at the masked men. Being in the game a minute, he knew if a nigga came up strapped with a mask, most times he would let you live. But if he were barefaced, then you had a ninety percent chance of being murdered. So, seeing the intruders with masks on motivated him to just give up the goods with no hesitation.

"The money and coke is up stairs in the hallway closet," he, said with blood running from his mouth.

Wallo took off up the stairs, taking three steps at a time. 40 could tell Wallo had either been in the house before or he was straight up stupid, not even checking to see who else was in there. Nor did he check Man-Man for a gun. 40 jut played his position, watching his victims on the floor.

Moments later, Wallo came down stairs and carrying two bags. "Pay Day, nigga!" he screamed.

Right then, two big ass German Shepherds came running out the kitchen, sending the room into a panic. They came straight at Wallo and 40. The brown-skinned dude that was sitting on the couch, hit the stairs like he was in the Olympics.

40 squeezed off three shots, stopping one of the dogs in its tracks.

Boom! Boom! Boom!

He then took off behind the dude who ran upstairs. Wallo wasn't so lucky. His Tech 22 didn't stop the other dog fast enough, jumping up and knocking him on his back. Wallo acted fast, putting his Tech 22 under the dog's stomach as he held him by the neck, stopping the dog from biting him. Then he let loose a stream of bullets into the dog's belly.

Tat, tat, tat, tat, tat, tat, tat!

The dog stopped fighting and fell over. 40 heard a crash in the bedroom on his right. He ran into the room and saw the window had been busted out. Looking out the window, he caught a glimpse of the dude limping before he jumped the fence in the back yard.

Tat, tat, tat, tat, tat, tat, tat, tat, tat!

40 could hear Wallo's Tech 22 still talking. By the time he made it back down stairs, the dogs, Man-Man and his baby moms were dead.

Chapter 7

Homicide Jack blew in his hands as he stood on the corner of 24th street. "Damn, it's nippy as a muthafucka out here. Where the fuck this little nigga at?" he said to himself, while he continued to blow in his hands, trying to keep them warm.

He scanned up and down 24th street discreetly. Nothing moved on the street he didn't fail to see. That was a habit that came with his trade of being a stick-up artist. Homicide Jack had many enemies, but he was feared by most of the hustlers in the streets of Newport News. He was the type of nigga that you didn't see that often or moved throughout the city. But whenever you did, it normally was because a homicide was taking place or a nigga was getting jacked. That's how he earned his name Homicide Jack.

Standing at 5'8", rocking a baldhead and goatee, Homicide Jack was a shinny dude that had a sense of sneakiness about himself. His jet-black skin was the color of motor oil. He possessed an enchanting pair of gray eyes that the ladies went crazy about, but he had a set of teeth that were so white, people thought they were fake. Particularly after having a bad habit of smoking and drinking coffee.

H looked down the block and saw a slew of crackheads standing in front of a house. He knew then the house was someone's trap house. He made a mental note to check it out if Lil BJ didn't show up. The horn of Lil BJ's car, however, caught his attention.

Beep! Beep! Beep!

"It's about time this nigga showed up," he mumbled to himself. Lil BJ pulled his Lexus up to the curb. He scanned his surroundings one last time, before getting into car.

"What's good, fam," he asked, extending his balled up fist to Homicide Jack for some dap.

"Just trying to get out the cold," he replied, bumping his fist. "I thought you weren't gon' show up for a minute. I was getting ready to shake the spot," he admitted.

"Nah, fam. I was definitely going to show up. I had to take care of a few things at the last minute," he told him, pulling away from the curb.

"So, what's the business?" Homicide Jack got right down to the reason he wanted to meet with him this morning.

"Damn, Jack. I thought I would at least take you shopping before we discussed the business, but I guess we can do it your way. I need some backing out here in these streets. I need somebody that can hold me down when shit starts to go haywire," he told him, stopping at a red light.

"Why you chose me? I feel like if a nigga out here in these streets can't govern what he got, then he don't deserve to have it " He eyed Lil BJ.

"Without a doubt I can hold my own. That's why I got what I have now. But a nigga got to have a strong team to keep what he got fam, and that's real talk. I want you to be part of that team, fam," Lil BJ spoke with sincerity, pulling off from the light once it turned green.

Homicide Jack nodded his head up and down, agreeing with him. He was feeling the little nigga's style. "Okay, so tell me the plan."

"I'm gon' need you to oversee the trap house until I get some workers. Once I get some, then you can manage them. But your main job will be watching my back," he said, making a left into MacArthur Mall.

"Hold the fuck up. How in the hell you got a trap house with no workers?"

"I been manning the trap house solo, but look, here are the figures. I'll pay you seventy-five hundred a week. That's thirty racks a month, three-hundred sixty a year."

Homicide Jack stuck his hand out for a handshake to seal the deal, then they hit the mall hard. Lil BJ bought his new crime partner everything from new socks, draws, T-shirts, boots sneaker, hygiene products, and leather jackets. He couldn't believe that this young nigga really was showing him this type of love.

"Man, lets head to the car and put the bags up before going back in to eat from the food court," Lil BJ suggested, helping him with the bags and shoeboxes.

"A'ight, lets do it then," he agreed, leading the way.

While loading the bags into the Lexus, a beautiful smoked-gray Benz truck whipped into the parking spot next to them. The sexiest woman eased herself out the SUV gracefully. When she started walking towards the mall, Lil BJ watched all that ass stuffed in her jeans. He knew right then he had to say something to the beau.

"Hey, baby girl," he called out. The girl turned half-way around, showing her Kodak smile.

"Hi," she replied, throwing up a manicured hand and waving.

"Can I holla at you for a minute?" he asked, walking her way. The beautiful dame stopped and waited for him to catch up with her.

Approaching her, Lil BJ could see she was a grown woman, not one of them hood bitches he was used to talking to. So right then and there, he knew he had to step his game up. "Hey, I'm Bryant. I was wondering if we could exchange numbers so we can get to know each other," he said, putting his best grown man act on. His heart was racing in his chest.

"What made you think I wanted to get to know you?" the woman said, throwing a hand on her hip and cocking it to the side like she had attitude. This gesture threw him off as he was at a loss for words. The woman then busted out laughing. "I'm just playing, Bryant. My name is Tashia. I would like to have your number, but you look kind of young, though. How old are you?" she asked, grabbing her phone out her Gucci bag.

"I'm old enough to fuck without getting stuck," he said with a smirk on his face.

"Boy, please. I'm going to give you my number because you're cute and I see you are on some grown man shit," Tashia stated, pointing to the gold Lexus she saw him loading bags in. "What's your number?"

"It's 703-399-3623," he replied, rattling off his digits off. Tashia punched the numbers in her phone and moments later, his phone begin to ring. He pulled the phone out his pocket and looked at the screen.

"That's my number right there, so save it in your phone. Nice to meet you," she told him before walking away. He stood there watching her ass with a big ole Kool-Aid smile, holding his dick through his jeans.

Chapter 8

Lil BJ made his way down Mercury Boulevard. He was incognito behind the tints of his 2008 Honda Accord. He parked his Lexus outside of his mother and sister's condo in Hampton. Everything had been running smooth for him and Homicide Jack.

They had recruited two of Homicide Jack's nephews, Moe-B and Lil Tate, to help run the trap house. Homicide Jack oversaw the management of it. With the fulltime presence of his nephews, the trap house brought in $800 a day. So Lil BJ agreed to pay them both $500 a day which $15,000 a month.

He was looking to expand his business, pulling into the Shell gas station and parking in the back. He pulled up next to Bugg's Tahoe and blew the horn. Bugg got out and made his way to the passenger side of the Honda, limping on crutches.

He eased into the Honda, gritting his teeth from the pain he was experiencing as he bent his leg to get into the small car.

"Man, what the fuck happened to you?" Lil BJ inquired.

"Lil BJ, you are not going to believe this shit. I was chilling over my partner Bean's house and out of nowhere, two muthafuckas come barging in the house with his baby moms at gun point. They had us dead to the right," he told him, shaking his head. "They were waving them hammers asking where the stash and money was at. My man Bean didn't even play games. He gave up that shit straight up with no problem. So when one of the gunmen came back with the stash, my man Bean's two German Shepherds came out the kitchen like Kojo. That's when all hell broke loose. Shots got to popping and I made it up the stairs, jumping out the second floor window to get away. That's how I fucked my leg up," Bugg told him, while dry swallowing some pain pills then firing up a blunt.

"So, what happened to your man and his baby moms?" Bugg let out smoke in between words.

"Man, them niggas kilt everything in that bitch. They killed my man Beans, his baby moms and the dogs." Bugg wiped a solo tear from his eye.

"Damn, fam. That's fucked up," Lil BJ said, shifting in his seat. They were both silent for a minute before Bugg broke the silence.

"Fam, I'm in the bind. Me and Bean was partners in this thang. But now he's gone and I'm real short on the re-up to purchase what I need to keep the hustle going." Bugg passed the blunt to Lil BJ, laying his head back on the headrest. "I'm gon' need about a hundred thousand for the next pick up." Lil BJ's mind was racing, thinking that this might be the expansion that he was looking for.

"Say I did come up with the money. What's in it for me?" Lil BJ asked.

"I will give you back the bread and you get twenty percent off the profit."

"How many joints you going to cop?" he inquired as he inhaled the weed.

"I'm getting forty-five joints," Bugg told him as he watched the gas station attendant dump trash in the dumpster, going back inside.

"I'll tell you what, Bugg. I'll give you the hundred thousand, but I meet the connect with you and we become partners all the way around."

"What! Nigga you got the game twisted!" Bugg spat with his face balled up.

Lil BJ was unfazed. "Take it or leave it," he said with a straight face. Bugg snatched the blunt out of his hand, took a hit and stared out the window for a moment.

"Sheesh! Lil BJ, you a fucking Jew, but I got to re-spect the game. It's a deal. From this day forward, we are partners. All our cards stay on the table," Bugg said firm-ly.

"I wouldn't have it no other way." He stuck out his hand so Bugg could seal the deal with a shake.

***

"Mama," seven-year-old Devon yelled from the front door at his mother who was having conversation with the next door neighbor in front of her duplex.

"What boy? You see me out here talking," Tashia yelled back at her son.

"Can me and Kevin have some juice and go in your room and watch cartoons on your TV?"

"Yeah, Devon. Now leave me alone," she told him, continuing her conversation with her neighbor.

Devon went to get he and his brother some juice. Kevin was right on his heels, making sure Devon poured the juice evenly. Heading to their mother's bedroom, their little feet pittered pattered across the floor. "We watching Sponge Bob?" Kevin asked, following behind his older brother.

"Yeah," Devon answered, searching the nightstand for the remote. When he couldn't find it, he walked over to his mother's dresser and went to a place she'd forbid-den him to be, including her closet. Not seeing the TV remote on the dresser either, Devon recovered a Bic lighter sitting next to a can of hairspray.

"Kevin, you want to see something?" Devon asked, picking up the lighter and hairspray off the dresser. Kev-in nodded his head up and down in response.

Devon then flicked the lighter, bringing a flame to the top of the lighter. He took the hairspray in his right hand and sprayed it over the flame of the lighter. The

41

flame ignited into a larger flame, creating a handheld flamethrower. Devon saw this in a movie he watched over his Auntie Tammy's house.

Whoosh, they heard as the flame roared.

Kevin jumped back a little and started laughing with his brother. Devon was holding the hairspray so close to the lighter, the small red button on the can of hairspray caught fire, burning Devon's little finger. Feeling the burning sensation, Devon flung the can out of his hand onto his mother's bed.

Whoosh!

The bed instantly caught on fire. Devon and Kevin raced to their room and played like that were both asleep, knowing their mother was going to beat their asses.

"Somebody's shit is on fire," Tashia said, smelling the smoke in the morning air. Glancing back over her shoulder, she saw smoke coming from underneath her front door.

"Oh my God! My babies!" she screamed, taking off in flight into her house. The neighbor ran to call the fire department.

Tashia couldn't see anything when she entered the burning house. The smoke was so thick. She fell to her knees and crawled throughout the house looking for her kids. "Devon! Kevin! Where y'all at?" They didn't answer, still playing possums in their beds with the covers pulled over their heads.

Tashia's heart pounded like an African drum. She made it to her kids' closed bedroom. She opened the door and found her babies in the bed. She ran to them and snatched them both out of bed. She made them crawl in front of her all the way to the front door. Getting outside, she hugged her boys tightly, rocking them back and forth in her arms. All she could think about now is all the money that was burning in bedroom closet.

Chapter 9
3 Months Later

"Oh shit, Bryant! Give me that dick, baby!" Tashia bit down on her bottom lip while she rode Lil BJ's dick smoother than a Mercedes ride. He grabbed a hold of Tashia's hips, pushing his pelvis into her, letting her have access to this full eight inches of dick. For him to only be seventeen, he was handling his business when it came to blowing Tashia's back out, giving her multiple orgasms.

Tashia worked her pussy muscles, tightening up her already glove-fitting love box around Lil BJ's stiff manhood. She could tell he was about to cum by the way his eyes began to roll in the back of his head. She knew then she had him right where she wanted him.

"You're going to cum for me?" she asked with a seductive voice.

"Un huh," he replied, letting out a deep breath.

"What you waiting for? Let me have it then," Tashia instructed him, speeding up her pace while bouncing up and down on his dick. They could hear her ass cheeks slapping up against his pelvis.

"Aghhhhhhhh!" he roared out.

Tashia slowed her pace as she fully laid her body on top of her lover, laying her head on his chest. Ever since the fire, Tashia and her kids had been staying with Lil BJ on the west side of Newport News. Tashia was there at first for the money, but over time Lil BJ's affection had won her over.

The way that he treated her was like no other man had dared treat her and on top of everything else, he was good to her kids. Tashia lost over $180,000 dollars in the fire. That was money left from the caper that set up

Skalez and 40 over a year ago which $310,000 was given to her for her role.

They were like two love birds. She was afraid to bring him around 40 and Wallo knowing they were robbing niggas again. She didn't want Lil BJ to get in their sights. "I love you, baby," she said as she kissed his lips. She brought her hips to a standstill, holding his manhood captive inside of her.

"I love you back, Tashia," he replied, kissing her back, while grabbing a handful of her ass to go with it. Tashia, for some reason, wanted to tell him about her past. She loved him so much she didn't want him hearing about her in the streets. She also didn't want to hurt him like that either. She hadn't felt this connected to a man since Skalez. Because of that, she just couldn't build up enough courage to share it now.

"How much you love me?" he asked her.

"I love you more than you could ever imagine." Tashia lifted her head from his chest to look him in his eyes.

"Would you die for me?" he asked.

Without hesitation, she replied, "Yes!"

Right then and there, she knew he didn't really mean she would actually have to die for him. He really was asking about her undeniable loyalty for him. He studied her eyes, searching for any falsehood, but didn't see any. He reached under the pillow he was laying on, producing a black rectangle box from Tiffany's. He handed it to Tashia who easily got off of his limp dick.

"What's this, Bryant?"

"It's something small that signifies your status in my life."

She opened the box and it contents made her jaws drop. Her love box started dripping all over again. Inside the box was the most beautiful chain and pendent she had ever seen. The pendent was a letter "B" with a crown sitting on top of it. The whole chain and pendent was crusted out in diamonds.

"Baby, no one has ever given me something like this." Tears started to build up in her eyes. Bryant took the chain out of her hands, getting hard and making her straddle him again. He then placed the chain over his lover's head. He admired how the "B" and crown rested nicely in between her perfect C-cups, the pink diamonds highlighting her brown skin. Tashia looked down at the gift Bryant gave her, then smiled at him.

"What got you all cheesing?" he playfully asked her, raking his fingertips up and down the smooth skin on her thighs.

"I guess you can call me Queen Bryant now," Tashia said playfully, batting her eyes.

"For sure," he seriously replied.

He hated breaking up this peaceful moment with her, but he had some moves to make. "Baby, a nigga would love to stay here all day and be in your guts, but I got to shake the spot. I need to meet up with Homicide Jack."

"I know, baby." Tashia let out a sigh. "But as a Queen Bryant, I must play my position and let you do what you do."

"Oh bitch, please. You couldn't wait to use the title Queen Bryant," he teased, bringing the couple to laughter.

She got up, allowing him to go take a shower. The last few months had been on a whole new level for Lil BJ. He met the connect Rio and made a good impression with him. Plus, the trap house has been jumping hard. Because of that, Lil BJ was no longer the name he was known by growing up. Now he was just BJ and he had the best coke on the side of the city.

After meeting the connect and seeing the high-grade product they were getting, BJ and Homicide Jack decided to sit down with Bugg. They suggested they not pollute the product with baking soda, instead selling it as is.

Bugg wanted to protest, but with Homicide Jack being present, he came into compliance. The product started moving faster and the money came in just as fast. This is exactly what Rio liked about BJ. He was a businessman. Making Homicide Jack top Lieutenant panned out to be useful for him, as well. He learned from him how the jack boys operated and how to always be alert and on point.

Homicide Jack taught him that someone was always watching, so he always needed to watch those who were watching you. He also convinced him to invest in a small arsenal and some bulletproof vests. He told him to always prepare for war in a time of peace. BJ stepped out the shower feeling like a King. Only if he knew that trouble was lurking.

Chapter 10

"Vanessa!" 40 called out to his sleeping beau that lay in his bed. Vanessa and 40 had met at a car auction a few months earlier. They were at odds bidding on the same car, a gold Lexus 400. 40 made a deal with her that if he backed off from the bidding, she would let him take her out to dinner. He only had plans to fuck her and send her on her way, but things were different when it came to her. She seemed to be of a different caliber of woman than what he was used to dealing with. But what was crazy was he knew she was straight out the hood. Still, her personality was captivating. She had that "lady in the streets, freak in the sheets" type of vibe and that alone made him keep her around.

Vanessa stirred in her sleep. Her 5'5" frame lay stretched across 40's bed. Her humbly round ass was exposed which he softly stroke. "Vanessa," he called her name again. Her light brown skin was creamy. She rolled over on her back after her buttocks was greeted by the warmth of his hand. Vanessa smiled at him and he smiled back, admiring her smile and voluptuous softball-sized breast. What enhanced her breast were her dark freckles that were dotted perfectly in between them.

"Good morning, boo," she replied, wiping the morning sleep out her eyes.

"Good morning to you, too. I woke you up to see if you were coming past the shops today."

"Awwww, you trying to make sure your woman's hair and nails stay tight, huh?" replied Vanessa. He wasn't ready to give her the title of his woman yet, but every day he spent they spent together broke down defensive walls down.

"You know that I can't have you running around Newport News with your feet and nails looking all

JIBRIL WILLIAMS

jacked up like the scarecrow off the *Wizard of OZ*," he replied, smiling.

"Oh yeah? You go jokes, nigga! You wasn't saying nothing last night when you was all in my pudding," she shot back, throwing a pillow at him he caught in mid air. He threw it back which started a pillow fight until his cellphone rang, interrupting their playtime.

Ring! Ring! Ring!

"Hello," 40 spoke into the phone.

"What's up, fam?" Wallo replied.

"I'm getting ready to head out to the shops. Buying the barber shop and beauty salon from Paula was a come up." 40 was bragging.

"I hear you, fam. I just wanted to ask if you heard anything about Skalez's situation?" Wallo asked.

"I haven't heard shit. It's like the streets not talking about it. Nobody knows shit," he said, walking out the bedroom as Vanessa lay there watching him.

"I've been getting the same results. Plus, Paula's not trying to give up that nigga name Skalez's killed before he died," Wallo told him, switching his phone to his other ear.

"I haven't heard from Paula since she moved to DC, but I tell you what, I'm going to holla at Skalez's moms. She might be able to give me the info I'm looking for," 40 told him, picking his Glock up he left on the living room table.

"When you do, let me know something, fam," Wallo said with sincerity.

"I will, bruh."

"Oh 40, I think I got us another lick line up, too." Wallo's voice went into a whisper.

"Line it up then. You know how we do," 40 said, laughing and disconnecting the call. "Yo, Vanessa. I'm gone. Are you coming by the shops?" 40 yelled from the living room.

"Yeah, boo. I'm coming by there after I take care of something for my brother, B."

"A'ight. When you do, bring me some lunch," he said, closing the door behind him.

JIBRIL WILLIAMS

Chapter 11
4 hours later

"Girl, I'm so fucking tired. My hands hurt like shit. How much coke we got to cut and bag up? We been going for hours," Trici complained, dropping a razor on the cutting plate and slouching down in her chair.

"I know, Trici. I was thinking the same thing. BJ gotta hire some more people to help us do this. I can't be doing this shit all day. I need to get down to Heavenly Fashion Beauty and Nail salon to get my nails touched up," Vanessa said, stuffing a 20 piece of coke into one of the small Ziploc bags that was laying on the table.

"Bitch, who in the hell you trying to fool? You trying to get down to the salon so you can chase all the bitches out of 40's face," Trici said, smirking at her friend.

"Oh yeah, that too!" she replied, bringing both ladies to laughter.

"I know that's right," she said, giving Vanessa a high-five. "But what's going on with you and 40 anyway? I mean is he breaking you off?" she inquired, being nosey as usual.

"Oh, without a doubt! My boo be wearing these goodies out!"

"I'm not talking about no dick, girl. I'm talking about money. Is he lining your pockets with some money, Vanessa?" Trici inquired again, getting all in girl's business.

"Yeah, he looks out for me, Trici, if you must know. But I have my own money and BJ does a good job of taking care of his big sister," Vanessa said, rolling her neck.

"What you mean he looks out for you? You call getting your nails and hair done looking out for you? Vanessa, you can get your own nails and hair done," Trici told her, trying to make something out of nothing with the conversation. "Don't you want your own money? You ever thought about being independent where you don't have to depend on no nigga or you brother to take care of you?"

"Yeah, who wouldn't want to not depend on any-one?" Vanessa replied, sealing another crack bag.

"Girl, I'm going to have my own money, even if I got to get it the grimy way," she spoke with a hint of seri-ousness in her voice as she got up from the table. That statement she made sent Vanessa's antenna's up, but she didn't comment on it. Then they heard someone knock-ing on the door, sending them into panic mode as coke laid across the coffee table broken into 20 and 50 pieces.

Knock, knock, knock.

"Who the fuck is that?" Vanessa asked, scooping the product into a shopping bag.

"I don't know," Trici replied, making her way to the front door. "Who is it?"

"It's a pizza delivery," a male voice said from the other side of the door.

"Pizza? Vanessa, did you order a pizza?" Trici asked, peeking through the peephole at the pizza delivery guy holding a red pizza delivery pouch.

"No, I didn't order a pizza. Trici don't open—" was all she said before Trici opened the front door. Every-thing else after that happened so fast once three masked men rushed into the house waving guns.

"Get the fuck on the floor, bitch!" one of the gunmen said, pushing Trici on the floor by her face. The other two gunmen immediately started raking the coke off the table and putting it in the same bag Vanessa was already using earlier. They even grabbed the cutting plate, scales, bags and razors and just as quick they came, they were gone.

"I think we should open up another trap house up," BJ said to Homicide Jack, sitting in Homicide Jack's 2008 Buick. They sat on the block watching the flow of traffic to and from the trap house.

"What's the purpose, BJ?"

"The purpose is to slow some of this traffic down. If we sell the twenties here and sell the fifties, two or three blocks over, it will split the traffic up." Homicide Jack smiled.

"I like how you think, BJ. I see you're getting sharp out here in these streets. But you know you're going to have to hire more people to run the new spot."

"Naw, that's your job. You're my top lieutenant. Whoever you hire, I don't want to meet them." The ringing of BJ' s phone interrupted the conversation. "Hello."

"BJ! They robbed us," Vanessa yelled hysterically through the phone.

"What! Who! Slow down, Vanessa! What happened?" BJ strained to hear his sister crying over the phone.

"Bruh, they robbed me!"

"Where you at?" BJ asked through clenched teeth.

"At Trici's house!"

"Sit tight. I'm on my way."

They pulled up at Trici's house on Coliseum Drive. The raggedy house had seen better days. BJ climbed the steps with Homicide Jack right on his heels. BJ walked in with out even knocking. Homicide Jack stayed posted by the door. When Vanessa saw her brother, she ran and jumped in his arms, crying her eyes out. "I'm so sorry, bruh."

BJ wrapped his arms around his sister and comforted her. "Tell me what happened from the beginning."

"We were bagging the work up," Vanessa said, sniffling and wiping her running eyes. "Then out of no where, someone knocked on the door. When Trici went to the door to see who it was, the person said they were here to deliver a pizza. After she opened the door, three masked men ran in here and took all the drugs."

Homicide Jack eyed Trici. Her body language told she had something to do with the robbery. She sat on the couch with her head hung low. She didn't even make eye contact with anyone in the room nor did she contribute anything to Vanessa's story.

"Why didn't you go to a hotel and bag the work up like I instructed you to do?" BJ asked his sister.

"We just felt more comfortable bagging it up here," Vanessa replied, now looking down at her feet. BJ just stared at his sister in anger. He had told her every time he gave her product, to bag it up using a different hotel.

BJ shook his head at his sister although he was grateful the intruders didn't harm her. "Come on, Vanessa. I'm taking you home," BJ said, leading his sister out the front door. Homicide Jack took a moment to stare Trici down before he left behind his boss.

Chapter 12

"Butta, don't get too close to that nigga. We don't want him to see us," Toflon said from the back seat of the navy blue Dodge van that Butta was driving.

"I got this, Toflon," Butta told him, keeping four cars behind them. "Damn, them niggas had a lot of yay in there." Butta started getting excited, thinking about all the coke him and Pookie raked off the table in Trici's house. "How much y'all think that shit was?" Butta asked, making a left off of Mercury Boulevard.

Toflon stared at the back of Homicide Jack's Buick intensely. "I think it's about two bricks or more."

"Do you think that Trici knows robbed her?"

"Man, right now fuck that bitch. I got her. She was taking too long to set something up. She was supposed to be getting some info on BJ and some nigga name 40, but shawty kept putting shit off. So, I had to make a move for the team." Toflon sat up and dug in his pocket to pull out a lighter to light his cigarette. He felt bad about robbing Trici. He was really starting to feel her. "Now, all we got to do now is follow BJ to the money," he told Butta, inhaling the Newport.

***

The silence in the Buick was tense. "What you think, Homicide Jack?" BJ asked, breaking the silence. Homicide Jack let out a long sigh.

"Pssss, I don't believe in coincidence," he replied, checking the rearview mirror. "This was a inside job, BJ. Look at how it went down. The robbers knew the drugs were in the house. They came in and went straight for the work. They didn't even check for any money. They didn't search the house. They just came in and snatched the work and hauled ass."

BJ nodded his head in agreement, taking in what Homicide Jack was telling him.

"Then you got to look at Trici. The entire time Vanessa was crying her eyes out, Trici never said anything. Not one peep," Homicide Jack continued, stopping at a red light. "I hate to say it, Vanessa, but your girl had her hands in this," he told her, looking at her through his rear mirror.

Vanessa just shook her head as a tear rolled down her face. Vanessa couldn't do anything, but think about her friend's comment earlier, *I'm going to get my own money even if I got to get it the grimy.* Vanessa knew then that everything Homicide Jack had just said made sense.

"Damn, two bricks!" BJ said out loud, rubbing the peach fuzz on his chin.

"Yo, fam. Hold tight. I think that blue van is following us," Homicide Jack warned him, making a right at the next corner, while nonchalantly keeping his eyes on the blue van that was three cars behind them. Sure enough, by the time he made it halfway down the block, the van made a right turn behind them.

BJ laid his head on the headrest and eyed the passenger side mirror. "Make another right," BJ said, slipping his p89 Ruger off his hip. "Vanessa, when I tell you to get down, get all the way down." BJ checked the gun to make sure that he had one in the chamber. Homicide Jack made right and the van followed right behind them.

"Okay, this the game plan," BJ advised them. "Go down about two blocks. There's an alley. Pull over at the lip of the alley. I'm going to hop out. If whoever in the van slows down or look our way, I'm letting them have it."

"A'ight, lets do it," Homicide Jack agreed. Vanessa's heart was racing. She wanted to turn around so bad and look out the back window, but she was paralyzed with fear. Entering the second block, BJ spoke to Vanessa without turning his head.

"A'ight, sis. Hit the floor."

Vanessa eased her body to the floor of the Buick and balled up into a fetal position. Homicide Jack pulled his gun and sat it on his lap. Seeing the lip of the alley BJ was talking about, Homicide Jack tapped the accelerator with his foot, whipping the car to the right and stopping a few feet from the alley way. BJ jumped out gun in hand, side-eyeing the Dodge van coming down the block. Homicide Jack cracked the driver's door for a quick exit in case he needed some assistance.

The van cruised by the both of them without breaking their speed. BJ stared hard at the van trying to get a glimpse of its occupants, but couldn't see inside due to the tints. But what was odd was him seeing a silhouette of someone sitting in the back seat.

***

"Damn, you see that? The bitch Vanessa just slumped down on the back seat," Butta said, turning the radio down a notch. "Then them niggas pulled over."

"Don't stop. Keep it moving. They on to us, fam," Toflon instructed Butta as they both clutched their burners, watching BJ jump out the Buick starting them down as they rode by. "You got lucky, playboy," Toflon mumbled as he watched BJ from his passenger mirror.

Chapter 13

40 sat in front of the salon smoking some Kush that was rolled tightly in a blunt. He was proud of himself for purchasing the businesses from Paula. The money that came from the shops was amazing. 40 made four to five thousand dollars a day. He saw why Skalez wanted to get out the game and go legit. He also remembered what Skalez shared with him and Block the night they robbed Lance.

"I'm about to be a father now, so I gotta take precautions at whatever I do," Skalez stated, standing in the hotel with a hand full of money.

"I know I will triple it, so I'm looking to use this money to invest in something instead of blowing it on bullshit," he added seriously. "I gotta be there for my little one. We grew up fatherless. Shit, the streets was our father. That's who raised us and I'll be damned if I don't be there for my child.

We all needed guidance but didn't have it. So what did we do? We went to the streets and got it the only way we knew how. My mother taught me how to be a good individual and all, but she couldn't teach me how to be a man. I am who I am, but now I'm down for a change because it's necessary."

Tap, tap.
Hearing the taps on the car window brought 40 out of his daydream. He looked at Vanessa's face smiling at him from the outside of the car. He hit the power locks on his black Beamer. She got in the car and let her round behind sink into the butter-soft seats.

"Hey, handsome," she greeted him as she leaned over and placed a wet one on his lips.

"Shit, Nessa. You tell me. You were a no show yesterday. I was waiting for you to come through and get your nails and hair done," he replied, returning her kiss.

"Some crazy shit jumped off with my brother yesterday." Vanessa laid her head back on the headrest and took a deep breath. It was clear to him something was bothering her, sensing it.

"So, what jumped off with your brother?" 40 inquired. She wasn't sure if she wanted to expose her brother's business, but she wanted 40 to know she wouldn't keep anything from him.

"Me and my girl Trici, I told you about was handling some business for my brother when some people bomb rushed her house and robbed us."

40's face frowned when Vanessa mentioned she was robbed.

"Wait, hold up, Nessa. They robbed you?"

"Yeah, that robbed us."

"What did they take?" he questioned, sensing she was holding back something.

"They robbed us of my brother's drugs we were bagging up for him."

"Damn, your brother got you bagging up for him?"

"No, baby. It's not what you think. My brother doesn't trust a lot of people, so he chose to keep his circle small. I just happen to be part of his small circle.

"What's your brother's name any way?" 40 adjusted his weight in his seat.

"Bryant. I don't think you know him. He is younger than us. He's out of a different age group," she said, watching a fat chick get out a green Honda with a dress on that was so tight, you could see every fat roll and pot hole her body had to offer. Vanessa just shook her head at the woman.

"But you straight though, right?" 40 asked, looking Vanessa in the eyes and stroking her face.

"Yeah, I'm alright," she replied, kissing 40's hand.

"Good, now lets go get that head done 'cause now you look like a nappy-headed bank robber," he teased her, laughing.

"Well, these hairs on this pussy ain't nappy," she shot back at 40.

"That's because I beat the naps out of them every chance I get," he said, laughing getting out the car.

***

"I can't believe you did that shit, Toflon!" Trici screamed. "I told you I was going to put something together for us!" Trici stood in front of Toflon upset with her hands on her chunky hips.

"Calm the fuck down! You were dragging your fucking feet. Me and my team got to eat. Plus, I did this for us. Every week you keep telling me to hold up. It's always about us, ma. You know that, right?" Toflon wrapped his arms around Trici, hugging her and gripping a handful of her ass. His touch made her melt.

"BJ and that crazy looking nigga Homicide Jack was looking at me all funny. What about them?" she asked, while her face was buried in Toflon's neck.

"Fuck them bitch as niggas. They don't have a clue you know who jacked them, so you in the clear, baby. It's anybody's instinct to think it's someone close to them," Toflon replied.

Trici wasn't too sure about what he was saying, but she had to believe in her man. He grabbed her face and kissed her gently. She moaned with pleasure while sucking on his tongue, igniting a flame in his manhood. It made him rise, becoming hard as a roll of quarters.

Trici found his hardness and stroked it through his jeans. She loved how thick he felt in her hand. She unbuckled his jeans, releasing his python-sized manhood.

61

She instantly descended to her knees and wrapped her mouth around Toflon's flute. Trici viciously bobbed her head up and down on him, letting her saliva coat his dick. She made slurping sounds with her mouth like they do in the porn movies. Her head game was on the point. It was like she had worked in a giving head clinic all her life.

Trici spit his dick out her mouth and grabbed his mushroom-shaped head, licking him up and down his shaft. Toflon's eyes rolled in the back of his head with pleasure. She placed his whole sack in her mouth and sucked him gently while stroking him. This technique sent him to his tippy toes, making his toes crack in the process.

"Damn, Trici. What you tryna do? Lock a nigga down?' Toflon asked, staring down at his human dick eater, while clutching the back of her head.

"Mmmhmm!" Trici moaned, still holding his sack in her mouth. She put him back in her mouth and begun sucking and jacking him at the same time.

Toflon started rocking back and forth in her mouth, giving her face a good fucking.

Every time he had these hardcore encounters with her, the hardness around his heart started to chip away. Toflon wanted to feel Trici's insides. He pulled out of her mouth in mid-stroke and snatched her off her knees.

Lifting up her T-shirt, he stared at her. He was used to seeing her in a nightgown. She didn't have on any panties. He turned her around and commanded her to grab her ankles, which she did without delay. She opened herself wide, waiting for the package only Toflon could deliver. He found her womb and entered her, giving Trici a strong thrust. .She had to remove her hands from her ankles, placing them on the floor to maintain her balance. Toflon started stroking her long and hard.

"Oh, Toflon. I'm cumming!" she screamed, releasing her load on his jungle stick.

He looked down as sweat dripped down his face. He watched his dick slam in and out of her. Her thick syrup-like juice coated him. This vision excited him, bringing him over the top.

"Here it comes, Trici," he announced, slamming harder into her big, round soft ass. He pulled out and spilled a walnut-sized load all over her backside.

Chapter 14

BJ and Tashia pulled up at Magic City strip club off of Jefferson. Tonight was a special night for him. It was his eighteenth birthday. Tashia had plans to make her man's birthday the most memorable one he would ever have in his life.

She rented out the strip club with some of the baddest bitches that they had to offer. She couldn't believe that BJ was only seventeen. When he finally told her his age, she wanted to be mad at him, but he loved her on a grown man level and his money and dick game were the truth. They pulled up and got out a money green Charger with black Ashanti rims which was a birthday gift that she persuaded BJ to buy.

Tashia look like she just stepped off the cover of a Straight Stunna Magazine, rocking an all white one-piece Prada tube dress. The form-fitting dress hugged her body so tight that one would think it was naturally part of her skin. She had to give it a tug here and there as she walked around the car to let BJ out on the passenger side. Her white red bottoms clicked clacked as she strutted her stuff. The pink diamond letter B chain rested peacefully on her chocolate skin as it lit up the parking lot.

She opened the passenger door and BJ stepped out wearing all black Gucci slacks and a black button down Gucci shirt. Everything was custom fitted, something Tashia took pride in having done for him. The red and green belt highlighted the Gucci slip ons that he wore. BJ set his whole outfit off with the crusted out Gucci watch with the red, green and black band. Tashia kissed BJ on the cheek as she laced her arm in his and lead him towards the Magic City entrance.

JIBRIL WILLIAMS

They walked in Magic City and were met by security. "We need to see your invitations, then pat you down," the burly bouncer said to them as they walked in.

"I don't think so," Tashia said. "This is our party and we don't do pat downs," she replied, pulling a V.I.P card out her epicurean-sized breast. Upon seeing the red VIP card, the bouncer let them in.

BJ smiled like a fat kid who loved cake when he saw all the beaus wearing white thongs with the letters "BJ" stamped on the front of them. The ladies were from all creeds of life. The "Happy Birthday" banner that hung in the middle of the club was a picture of Tashia naked with a "Happy Birthday" sign in front of her breast and love box. BJ found the picture to be hypnotizing.

The party was an all white affair. The only person allowed to wear any color other then white was BJ. Tashia had set strict rules. If the person didn't wear white, whether they got an invitation or not, and even if they were a female, they could only get in being butt ass naked. That was the only alternative.

Tashia led BJ to a corner table where two beautiful Asians twins came over topless, carrying four bottles of champagne. Their small pinkish nipples were perky as both women spoke in unison. "Happy Birthday, BJ!"

BJ nodded with a smile. Not wanting to disrespect his woman, he diverted his eyes away from the twins. Tashia watched BJ intensely. Picking up on his unwillingness to look at the two babes standing before him, she grabbed his crotch through his Gucci slacks.

"Don't look away. Tonight is your night. Enjoy yourself, baby." BJ look into her eyes for any trickery and found nothing but two pair of lustful eyes staring back at him. He grew in her hand.

"Damn, baby. You did all this for me, huh?" He then took a sip of the champagne straight from the bottle.

"You deserve every bit of it. This is your night." Tashia stroked her man's ego and manhood.

"Yo, fam. What's good!" Moe-B said, walking up with Lil Tate. "I see you got this muthafuka looking right, fam. Happy birthday, nigga."

"Thanks, Moe-B." BJ stood up and hugged Homicide Jack's two nephews.

"Thanks, fam!" BJ embraced his workers and sat back down, passing Moe-B and Lil Tate a bottle of Dom P. "Drink up, niggas. It's on me tonight!" he yelled, raising a bottle of champagne in the air. Tashia had invited the entire city of Bad News to come out to help bring his birthday right.

"Whoa, it's some bad bitches in here tonight, fam," Moe-B said, eyeing a tall light-skinned chick that walked by their table who had "Happy Birthday" airbrushed across her 48-inch ass, another one of Tashia ideas.

"Yo, where that nigga Homicide Jack at? I know his old ass ain't missing out on a party like this?" Lil Tate asked excitedly, looking at all the woman prancing and dancing around the club.

"I got him on some shit right now, but he'll be here in a minute," BJ replied.

"Baby, I got to go check on a few things," Tashia whispered in BJ's ear before she passed him a few ounces of Kush and few boxes of Atimos.

"A'ight, baby. I'm gon' be right here doing me." When Tashia got up, he smacked her on the ass. Moe-B watched her ass in lust, something BJ noticed. He made a mental note to test Moe-B later on down the line.

***

"Man, it ain't shit in this muthafucka," 40 said with aggression as he cut open the cushions on the couch. "We've been in this bitch for about twenty minutes."

"Fam, I know shit is in here. We just got to find it," Wallo replied as he watched a spider crawled into a crack in the baseboard behind the TV. Wallo walked over to get a better look at the baseboard. He then stuck his finger in the three-inch crack and pulled. Then the baseboard fell away from the wall.

"Got it," he said out loud, stopping 40 from his search. Packed nice and neatly in the lining of the baseboard was nothing, but green backs of them dead presidents.

"It's about time, Wallo. I was about to give the fuck up." 40 admitted.

"You should know better then anybody that you have to be patient when it comes to these type of missions." Wallo started loading the money into the duffle bag. It looked to be one hundred and fifty thousand.".

"I know that work in here," Wallo said, standing up from the baseboard.

"Man, fuck the work. We got the money," 40 told him, walking towards the back door they kicked in to gain access into the house.

***

"Look at what the cat done drag in!" Tashia said, walking up to Vanessa.

"Tashia, don't hate because I'm rocking my Prada dress better then you," Vanessa replied with a smile on her face. Her and Tashia shared a laugh.

"Whatever. You look good, though," Tashia replied, giving Vanessa her props.

"Thanks, Tashia. Happy Birthday, bruh." Vanessa gave BJ a hug. "Damn, I see Tashia got ass everywhere in the bitch."

"Thanks, sis. You know Tashia was going to do it up for her man," he bragged, filling a flute full of champagne for his sister.

The lights in the club blinked off and on with red and blue. An Amazon-like stripper wearing knee-high black leather boots and an airbrush paint on the ass of a picture of BJ brought Tashia a micro-phone. The woman looked at Tashia seductively, walking to a back room. BJ's dick jumped in his Gucci slacks as he watched the stripper's ass cheeks clap with authority as she walked away.

"Okay, everybody," Tashia said, being heard throughout the club as she spoke through the mic. "It's time to sing Happy Birthday for my baby." Two exotic looking dancers pushed a huge cart with a cake on it towards them. When BJ saw the cake, a smile appeared across his face. The cake bore a picture of a pussy.

Tashia started the Happy Birthday chant and the whole club followed. "Now, come and get a slice of this pussy. This will be the sweetest pussy you will ever taste," she yelled through the mic, making the club laugh. At that moment, BJ realized that the pussy that was on the cake was Tashia's.

The big brute figured bouncer came and whispered in BJ's ear. "Man, we have a problem at the door." BJ signaled for Moe-B and Lil Tate to follow him. Tashia and Vanessa fell right in line behind them. Getting to the door and stepping outside, BJ was met by Toflon and his men. "What's the problem, fellas?" he asked, popping the cuffs of his shirt.

"Man, we trying to get in, but these bitch ass flashlight cops ain't trying to let a nigga in," Toflon spoke aggressively in BJ's face. Moe-B and Lil Tate stepped up beside him. Moe-B put his hand on Toflon's chest and gave him a little push back. Toflon knocked his hand away. Then Moe-B placed his hand on his gun.

"Listen, fam. This is a private affair. The rules are the rules. You don't have on white, you can't get in and plus you wasn't invited," BJ informed Toflon.

"Man, I don't give a fuck about no private party. I want to drink and see some hoes," Toflon said, getting back in BJ's face.

BJ scanned the parking lot of the club and saw all eyes were on him. He turned to Tashia and whispered in her ear. Tashia immediately disappeared, going back inside the club. BJ had to play it cool because everyone was watching him. He couldn't let things get out of hand on his birthday. "I'm going to meet you in the middle." On que, Tashia came out the club holding three bottles of Moet. "I'm going to give you a drink and it's on me," he said as she handed Toflon and his men a bottle a piece.

"Cool, but what about seeing some bitches?" Toflon asked, reaching and grabbing one of Tashia's thick ass cheeks. BJ grabbed him with so much force, Toflon's hand fell off of her ass.

"It looks like we got us a problem here," Homicide Jack said, walking up and pointing a chrome Bulldog 44 at Toflon. Toflon looked unfazed. "I asked do we have a problem here?"

Homicide Jack stepped closer, putting his gun to Toflon's head and cocking the hammer. The crowd that was outside started to fade farther into the parking lot. He stared at Homicide Jack with murder in his eyes, but he wasn't no fool. He would live to fight another day.

"You got that, O.G.," Toflon mumbled, spinning on his heels and walking away.

Back in to club, Tashia could tell BJ's partying mood was thrown off by the situation that just took place outside the club. It was time for her to give him her birthday present. She headed to the back where the private rooms were. Twenty minutes later, BJ was summoned to the private room where he found Tashia and the stripper they called Amazon.com. Both were lying on a bed feeding each other fruit. Now he was ready to get his birthday candle blown out.

Chapter 15

"Man, from now on we on them nigga's asses," Toflon spoke from the back seat of Butta's Dodge van.

"Man, I'm telling you we should wait for the party to be over, then get the real party started right there in the parking lot," Pookie said from the passenger seat.

Toflon was heated. Never in his 25 years of living had a nigga ever pulled a gun on him. He made it his business to kill BJ and Homicide Jack once he caught them slipping. "Naw, we're going to hold up on that. I got some better plans. We're going to do this right. We're going to take everything them niggas got," he stated with malice in this voice.

"Yo, fam. The old head nigga is Homicide Jack. I heard a lot of shit about him. They say fam is an animal in these streets. So, we got to be on point when we fucking with him." Butta then made a right on Jefferson.

"Man, fuck Homicide Jack's washed up ass. That nigga is a has been. We are the shit now," Toflon shot back, balling his face up.

"Oh shit! The police just got behind us." Butta sat straight up behind the wheel. He eased the radio down and kept going straight down Jefferson. "Damn, I hope that these muthafukas don't pull us," Butta spoke out loud, watching the law in his rearview.

"Shit!" Toflon yelled out. "Man, make a right in that shell gas station!"

Butta made the right into the gas station. The police car made the same right behind them. "Damn, fam. They on us," Butta told them, pulling next to gas pump four.

Pookie was quiet as a snitch at a gangsta party. He had just gotten out of prison from doing two years and anything that led to him going back wasn't sitting well with him. The police car drove past them, pulling right up to the convenience store. When the cop got out and went in, the trio in the van let out a sigh of relief at the same time.

"Man, get me the fuck to my girl's house. Shit crazy out here tonight," Toflon said, wiping the sweat off his forehead. He was relieved the police weren't about to pull them over.

Trici had sunk her hooks into Toflon. He found himself spending most of his time with her. He didn't know what transpired over the last two months, but she had become his chocolate chip to his chocolate chip cookies. And every time he entered in her and she moaned his name, he fell deeper into her web.

Riding in Butta's van with three guns, almost being stopped by the police and having a gun placed in his face was enough close encounters for Toflon in one night. He was ready to go home to Trici. It was time to end his night smoking weed with Trici bouncing up and down on his dick. Butta pulled up in front of her house. Toflon dapped his partners up.

"I'll get with you niggas tomorrow," he told them before he got out the van, sliding the door close. He walked to the front door noticing the living room lights were on. He let himself in the house with the key that Trici had given him.

"Trici, where you at?" Toflon called out, not getting an answer. He noticed the TV was on, so he made his way to the back of the two-bedroom house. Something didn't seem right to him, so he eased his Sig 45 off his hip. Turning the doorknob to Trici's bedroom, he pushed the door open with ease. His eyes scanned the room. He smiled seeing Trici lying on her stomach and her big ole dookie up in the air.

He closed the door and began to creep out of his clothes. The moonlight that shined through the window and bounced off her ass alone made Toflon hungry to be

74

inside of her. Standing at the foot of the bed, Toflon stroked himself to a full erection. Crawling on top of her, he pushed his stiffness into her and began to slowly stroke her. "Hey, baby. Daddy's home," he whispered in her ear.

Trici didn't acknowledge his manhood invading her womb nor did she respond to his verbal announcement. Toflon pumped a little harder trying to get a reaction out of her. He laid his head against the side of her face and felt a wet sticky substance. "What the fuck!" Toflon jumped off her and wiped the side of his face. "What the fuck is this?" he asked himself. "Trici!" he yelled, calling out her name out louder. Not getting a response, he hit the switch on the lamp that sat next to the bed. The light-filled room brought horror into his world. Trici lay there on her bed butt naked with the back of her head blown out.

***

"You stood me up, Robert. You promised me that you were going to make it to my brother's birthday party," Vanessa said with an attitude through the phone. 40 hated she used his government name.

"Look, Nessa. Some shit came up and I had to shoot to P-Town on the other side of the bridge," he told her. "Vanessa, I promise you, I will make this up to you and your brother," he pleaded.

"It's okay, Robert. Don't even bother. It's getting late. I'm going to leave the now and head home," she said still keeping her attitude.

"I'm going to come through and holla at you tonight," he replied.

Vanessa let out a sigh. "I'll just catch up with you tomorrow," she stated sternly, disconnecting the call."

JIBRIL WILLIAMS

Chapter 16

BJ opened his eyes and stretched in his bed. The amazon stripper from Magic City lay next to him. He smiled as he thought about last night with Tasha and the stripper. *Damn, my baby was a straight freak last night, BJ thought* to himself. He reached over and palmed the stripper's ass and shook it, making it shake like Jell-O. "Yeah, that bad boy is real because that fake shit don't shake like that," he whispered. She giggled and rolled over, facing him with a smile.

"Hey, birthday boy," she spoke with a southern drawl in her voice.

"What's up, rna. Where is Tashia?" Smelling the smell of bacon in the air, BJ already knew where she was. "Never mind, shawty. Get some rest," he told her.

"Are you sure?" she asked, grabbing a hold of his fat member and stroking him.

"Yeah, I'll be back to take you up on that offer," he said, prying her hands from around his dick. He jumped up and threw on a pair of sweat pants, making his way to the kitchen. He found Tashia standing over the stove wearing a small T-shirt and a pair of white thongs. He admired her rear with an appreciation.

"Thanks for the party last night," he said, walking behind her and wrapping his arms around her. He then cupped her fat muffin that was struggling to bust out the front of her thong.

"You are welcome, baby." Tashia pressed her ass against his manhood while he placed a kiss in the crock of her neck. She then started grinding on his manhood.

"I didn't know you got down like that, baby," he whispered, referring to the threesome that she blessed him with last night.

"Well, to be honest with you, I have dibbled and dabbled with exploring my sexuality in the past, but last night was strictly for your pleasure only."

"I appreciate the fact you shared that with me and just for the record, you gave me my first threesome," he confessed. "You know, I feel so comfortable with you."

"That's how it should be, baby." Tashia turned around to face her lover. "I feel the same way, BJ. There are so many things I need to tell you about me."

"So tell me, baby," he replied, kissing her on her chin. Tashia hesitated, searching his eyes for any sign of judgment.

"Good morning!" the amazon stripper spoke after entering the kitchen fully dressed.

"Hey, Meka! You hungry?" Tashia asked her.

"Yeah, can I just have a sandwich to go? I want to go home get some rest. I need to get my hair done later before I head back to the club," she replied, eyeballing Tashia's thick thighs. BJ gritted his teeth about the missed opportunity to fuck the Amazon stripper one last time before she left.

"I don't think I properly introduced you two. This is my boo, BJ. BJ, this is Meka, but in Magic City, she's Ms. Amazon.com," Tashia said with a smile.

"Nice to met you, BJ."

"And it's nice to meet you," he replied with a little slickness in his voice. Tashia made Meka an egg and bacon sandwich and put it on a napkin.

"Thanks, girl," Meka said, accepting the sandwich from Tashia. She then kissed her on the cheek while palming Tashia's ass cheek with her empty hand. She did the same to BJ, but instead of grabbing his ass, she grabbed a handful of dick.

Tashia walked her to the door to let her out. She quickly jumped back when she saw Homicide Jack standing there getting ready to knock.

WHEN THE STREETS CLAP BACK 2

"Oh shit!" she blurted out, standing behind the door. Homicide Jack saw her monkey trying to jump out the front of her thong. He quickly turned his back as if he didn't see anything. He had too much respect for BJ to look at her in that manner.

"I'm sorry, Tashia," he apologized.

"It's alright, Homicide Jack. I'm so embarrassed," she replied, moving to the side to let Meka out the door. He watched the stripper's ass dance from side to side as she made her way to her Audi.

"Give me a minute, Homicide Jack. I'll let BJ know you're here," she told him, closing the door. She made her way back to the kitchen, finding him flipping a pancake in the skillet on the store. "Baby, Homicide Jack is at the front door. I didn't let him in because I wasn't properly dressed."

"A'ight, go put some clothes on," he said, walking over and kissing her fully on the lips while pinching her on her gigantic butt.

"Ouch, BJ!" she cried out, trying to wiggle out of his grasp. He grabbed her firmly, getting her attention.

"Listen, baby. Later, I want to hear about everything you feel you need to tell me," he said sincerely, looking into Tashia's eyes. "And know whatever you tell me, I wont judge you."

Tashia squeezed BJ tightly. "Thank you, baby. We will talk later. I love you," she told him, giving him a kiss

"Love you back," he replied, letting her go so he could let Homicide Jack in.

"What's up, fam," he said, opening the door.

"You tell me, playboy!" Homicide Jack walked into the house embracing BJ. "Damn, we had fun last night."

"Shit, you? Man, I can't even begin to tell you how much fun a nigga had last night," BJ said, thinking about the awesome threesome he had last night. "So, how did things go?" he asked, changing the subject. He didn't want Homicide Jack to know much how much of a freak Tashia was for him last night.

"Everything went well and I found out who robbed Vanessa and Trici." Homicide Jack then took a seat on the cream color leather sofa.

"Who?" BJ asked, splitting an Atimo and rolling the Kush.

"It was a inside job. It was Trici's boyfriend. Some nigga named Toflon. She said she didn't know he was gon' rob her, but a bitch will tell you anything when there's a gun a in their face," he said, tossing BJ a lighter. "She also told me that she was supposed to get some info on a nigga named 40, so her boyfriend could rob him, too." Hearing 40's name made BJ pause and look at Homicide Jack. "What's the matter, fam?" he asked, looking at the expression on BJ's face.

BJ knew in life, there weren't any coincidence. There were only signs and warnings. He knew this situation was no other than a warning.

"Fam, I need you to handle some shit for me," BJ said, lighting the Atimo and inhaling the Kush. "The nigga 40, I need a hit as soon as possible," he spoke in between puffs.

Homicide Jack sat straight up on the sofa and asked one simple question. "Why?"

BJ let out a cloud of smoke. "40 killed my man Lil Chris' brother a few years ago. Then one night 40's man Skalez came and pulled me in on a lick. I went on the move with the nigga 40 while Skalez and their boy Block hit another location. But what was crazy is I know 40 came out that house with 2 bags of money. The nigga played me like a sucka. He gave me 5 stacks and sent me on my way." BJ took another hit of the Kush and passed it to Homicide Jack.

"So, you mad the nigga gave you five stacks?"

"Naw, it goes deeper than that. Like I said, 40, Skalez and Block killed my man's brother. They took a chain from him after they robbed and killed him. So when Lil Chris saw Block wearing his brother's chain at a club one night, he knew that Block killed him or at least had something to do with it. So, me and Lil Chris caught Block slipping and rocked him to sleep. We wanted to get 40, but he had went to jail for a gun charge and some drugs."

"So, what happened to your man Lil Chris?" Homicide Jack asked, passing a ashtray and the Atimo to BJ.

"I'm going to get to that," he said. "Me and Lil Chris ran in Skalez' house at gun point. We made him open the safe and give everything up." BJ hit the Atimo. "We both were slipping because we let him reach in the safe and pass us the money. This nigga Skalez wasn't going out like that. He reached in and pulled out a gun, hitting Lil Chris in the chest and killing him. I had to drop Skalez," BJ told him, looking into space as he visualized the whole event in his head.

"Damn, BJ. That sounds like some movie shit," Homicide Jack said, rubbing his chin. "So, basically you want 40 dead for killing Lil Chris and his brother?"

"Yeah and I got fifty stacks for the job, too," BJ replied, relighting the Atimo.

"A'ight, young blood. I can handle that for you," he said, agreeing to kill 40.

***

Tashia held her hand over her mouth in astonishment. Tears trickled down her face. She couldn't believe what she just overheard. BJ had killed a man that was once very close to her. She had to make a decision if she was going to let BJ kill 40 or not.

JIBRIL WILLIAMS

Chapter 17
2 Days Later

40 opened the black velvet box and stared at the one single item inside. He pondered if he was doing the right thing. He just could not see himself not having Vanessa with him twenty-four seven . He knew she was still mad at him for not showing up to her brother's birthday party, so he was hoping this gesture would get him back in her good graces.

He climbed out his 745 series, knocked some lint off his black jeans and double checked his fresh Air Force Ones for scuff marks. His white and black Polo shirt stopped just past his pockets to conceal the butt of his 45. 40 was a true street nigga, but Vanessa was bringing that soft side out of him.

He wondered at times was it because he lost everyone that meant something to him. He couldn't determine why he clung to Vanessa or if he in fact he really loved her. But one thing was for sure was the feelings he had whenever he was with her and he didn't want them to go away.

40 grabbed the two dozen of pink roses off the back seat and made his way to the front door of Vanessa's house. He hadn't been over there much since she stayed out Hampton in a gated community. He gave the door three solid knocks and waited.

"Who is it?" he heard her asked from behind the door.

"It's the love of your life," he replied, smiling.

"Oh, I don't have one of them," she teased, giving 40 a hard time as she watched him through the peephole. 40 didn't like that response.

"Vanessa, stop playing and open the door!" he told her, getting aggravated for playing when he was trying to do the romance thing with her.

She opened the door standing there wearing nothing but some pink, laced panties with a custom made T-shirt that read "I Love Robert". 40 smiled at the view Vanessa gave him. He could see the creases of her pussy lips through her panties and her erect nipples were on display though her shirt.

"Good morning, baby," 40 spoke, kissing her on the lips and handing her the pink roses.

"Wow, Robert. They are beautiful." Vanessa inhaled the sweet scent of the flowers and closed the door behind him as he walked in.

"I came by here to see if you wanted to go breakfast with me," he said.

"Are you sure you just came here to ask me to break-fast or are you trying to make up for not showing up to my brother's party?" he looked at her. .He knew she wasn't going to make it easy for him, so he choose to just keep it real with her.

"To be honest, Nessa, it's a little bit of both. I came here to ask you out on a breakfast date and to seek your forgiveness." 40 paused before he continued. "But I really came here to ask you a more important question." He got down on one knee and pulled the black velvet box out of his back pocket. "Vanessa, I hate waking up without you beside me. There's never a time I want to walk in the house and not see your smiling face. I want you near me twenty-four seven.", 40 opened the box and stared down at it contents.

Vanessa was shocked out her mind. She pranced around on her tippy toes while 40 spilled his soul to her. She still couldn't see what was inside the box yet.

She never thought she would get a proposal while wearing a pair of panties and a T-shirt while someone held two dozen of roses. She began to cry.

"Vanessa, would you move in with me?" 40 asked, turning the velvet box around for her to see. Lying in the black velvet box was a key.

"What, a key? Robert, you play too many damn games." Vanessa hit him playfully on the shoulder, then gave him a quick kick to the side, knocking him completely on the floor. "Nigga, you don't get down on your knees unless you getting ready to eat pussy or to ask a bitch to marry you. Robert, you had me crying and everything." She kicked him a little harder as he held his side from laughter.

"I'm sorry, baby," 40 said through laughter. "I didn't it mean for that to happen like that." He smiled while she jumped on him and straddled him.

"I will move in with you, but when I'm ready." Vanessa started grinding on 40. She could feel his manhood coming to life between her legs. She lifted up and undid 40's jeans, pulling his love muscle free. She pushed her panties to the side and eased down on his throbbing dick.

"Shit, Nessa!" he moaned in pleasure as her pussy rested on the base of his shaft. "When are you going to move in?" 40 asked, grinding his into her.

"Once my mom gets herself together and gets out of rehab," Vanessa said, biting down on her bottom lip. She went shortly after BJ moved them out and was making great progress.

***

"Homicide Jack, I'm pulling up at the Soap and Suds car wash on Mercury now," LJ told him..

"I'm in the Buick," he shot back and disconnected the call. He watched his long time comrade LJ climb out of his hooptie and made his way to his Buick.

"What it is?" LJ asked, getting into the car, giving Homicide Jack some dap.

"You the man!" Homicide Jack said with a smile. "Welcome home, nigga."

He passed a small brown bag to LJ that held a stack of small bills.

"Good looking out, my nigga!" LJ replied, giving him some dap. Homicide Jack put the Buick into drive and got in line to go through the car wash.

"You ready to get back in the game?" Homicide Jack asked.

"Badder than a muthafucka," LJ replied.

"Good, I need a hit done." Homicide Jack pulled behind a white Charger.

"Give me the run down."

Homicide Jack wiped the top of his baldhead. "You remember a little nigga that be out here putting down his stick up game? His name is 40." LJ searched his memory trying to put a face with a name. It sounded familiar to him, but it was hard placing the face the name.

"It's ringing a bell. Oh shit, hold up! I think I remember! He used to run tight with a nigga named Skalez," LJ said excitedly.

"Bingo!" Homicide yelled out." That's why he called on his old friend because he knew everybody in the city, big or small. That came with the type of service that he provided.

"Okay, what he do?" LJ inquired.

"I'm not in a position to discuss that." Homicide eased his car on the track to go through the automatic washer. "But I can tell you that the job pays twenty thousand large."

WHEN THE STREETS CLAP BACK 2

"Shit, you don't have to tell me shit. The price tag alone done said enough," LJ told him, rubbing his hands together.

"Alright. I need this done soon as possible. I don't have any leads on 40, but finding a nigga is your specialty. I'm going to let you handle that."

Homicide Jack reached in the back seat, grabbed a black shaving kit bag and gave it to LJ. He looked in the bag and saw two of the prettiest 45s.

"These are yours and they're clean," he advised him as the Buick came out of the automatic washer.

"Good looking, Homicide Jack. I need this job."

"If you handle this properly, I'm going to introduce you to my little man," he said, giving LJ some dap.

"I'm on it, bruh!" he replied, getting out the Buick and hopping into his hooptie and leaving the wash. Homicide Jack smiled to himself knowing that he just unleashed a monster on 40's ass.

Chapter 18

BJ entered into Aymir's Jewelers. He wanted to purchase a little promise ring for Tashia. Lately, she'd been acting really distant. He even caught her crying on a few occasions. He didn't know if she was feeling guilty about the threesome she gave him or the fact he hadn't made time to sit down with her so she could bare her soul about her past. But whatever the situation was, he was concerned and he was going to do everything in his power to bring her out of her funk.

"May I help you, sir?" a beautiful white woman asked, smiling at BJ.

"Ummm, yeah sure! I'm looking for something like an engagement ring, but it's not technically a engagement ring." He replied, hoping the lady could understand what he was looking for.

"So, basically you're looking for a ring that will temporarily lock your special someone down until you finally ask her the big question?" the white lady asked with a smile. But deep down inside, she disliked men like him that strung women along with a ring hoping some day they would marry them.

"Yeah, something like that," he confirmed.

"Ok. Come this way, please," she instructed BJ, taking him three display cases down.

"Here's something that might strike your interest," the sales clerk said, showing him a 2-karat diamond engagement ring. He examined it, but it wasn't what he was looking. Then after seeing the price tag, he knew the ring or the diamond in it weren't real.

"Naw, baby. This is that cheap shit. I want to real deal," BJ stated, handing the sales clerk the ring back. "Is there a manager that I can talk to?" he asked.

"Well, you are in luck. Aymir, the owner, is in his office. Would you like to talk to him, sir?" the sales clerk said sternly, feeling slightly offended that BJ asked for a supervisor

"Yeah, that would be cool." BJ caught the hint of aggravation in the sales clerk's voice. She then disappeared behind a curtain. Moments later, she came back with a Arab looking guy who rocked blue jeans and all white T-shirt like he was a hood nigga.

"Hello, I'm Aymir. How may I help you?" he asked, extending his hand to him to which BJ accepted.

"I'm good, fam. I'm looking for a little something for my lady. I just can't seem to find what I want or should I say find something that's deserving of my woman," BJ said with confidence.

"I think we can find just what you're looking for if you just step this way," Aymir directed him behind the counter and behind some curtains. Reaching Aymir's office, he admired the photos on the wall that bore him posing with different celebrities. "What can I help you with?" he asked, sitting behind his oakwood desk.

"I'm just looking for a semi engagement ring. Something that really says 'I love you' without saying it," BJ confessed.

Aymir smiled and pulled a blunt from out of his top drawer. "Do you mind?" he asked, holding the blunt in the air.

"Go ahead, playa. Do you. Shit, I smoke, too," BJ replied. Aymir put some heat to the blunt and took a couple of pulls.

"I just got some new pieces in yesterday that I think might fulfill your request." Aymir opened the bottom drawer on the desk and removed a black cloth tray. There were about 25 to 30 different rings. Aymir slid the tray towards him so he could get a better view of the merchandise. BJ took his time looking through the tray thoroughly. Then he saw one in particular that jumped out at him. He knew this was the ring for Tashia.

"I like this one right here." BJ grabbed the platinum ring with a 2-karat rock in it and held it in the air. The light bounced off of the diamond, putting him in a trance. Aymir was impressed with his selection.

"She's pretty, isn't she?" Aymir asked, passing the blunt and letting the smoke seep through his nose.

"Hell yea," he replied, accepting the blunt.

"The price tag on her is $8,559," Aymir told him .

"Alright, I got that for you." BJ stood up with the blunt hanging from his lips. He removed a baseball-sized knot from his pocket and pulled $8,600 from it, dropping it on Aymir's desk. "Put that in one of them black velvet boxes," he told him.

Aymir smiled, something he often did when he ran into customers that paid in cash.

"Hey, Brenda!" he yelled. Thirty seconds later, the white sales clerk stuck her head in the door.

"Yes, Mr. Aymir."

"Take this and polish it up real quick and place it in one of our custom designed boxes. Have it ready for my friend here."

"Ok, yes sir," Brenda replied, taking the ring from BJ and exiting the room.

"You know, my friend, I see that you like the weed," Aymir said, noticing he hadn't passed the blunt back to him. It just occurred to BJ he was being a hoover.

"Damn, my bad," he stated, passing the blunt back to Aymir who declined the it.

"Naw, that's you." Aymir stood to his feet. "Maybe in the near future, if you looking to cop some good bud, you come holla at me and I can point you in the right direction."

BJ nodded his head up and down, thinking to himself that he had just came up on a weed connect that easy. "A'ight, bet that up." He stood, giving Aymir his hand.

"By the way, the name is BJ." Aymir shook his hand firmly.

They walked to the front of the store where Brenda had the ring polished ready to go.

"Thank you, sir, " she said, handing him a small jewelry bag.

"Thanks for shopping at Aymir's Jewelers," Aymir said, handing him his personal card.

"Thanks, fam. I'll most definitely be getting back with you on that other situation," he said to Aymir, turning on his heels and walking out the jewelry store.

Chapter 19

Toflon had been drinking non-stop since he found Trici dead. The Henny and Kush he'd been drinking and smoking on had him thinking some evil thoughts. He knew in his mind BJ was behind the murder of his girl-friend, which was a consequence of him robbing him. "Sucka ass nigga killed my girl. Why the fuck he didn't come at me? I took the work," he spoke to himself out loud.

Grabbing the Mack 10 off the floor that rested be-tween his feet, Toflon started to load the deadly weapon with an expert precision despite the fact he was pissy drunk. He carefully wiped every bullet clean before he placed them in the clip. "Touch one of mines, I'm going to destroy everything you touch," he mumbled.

Trici's smiling face crept into his mind like an early morning fog. Her face was so vivid, so bright full of life. Toflon grabbed the neck of the Henny bottle and turned it up to his lips. He took big gulps, letting the liquid burned his throat on the way down. "Argggh!" he roared out, slamming the bottle down on the table and sitting in front of him. "Pookie! Butta! Lets ride, niggas."

Toflon wobbled, kicking Butta's feet who was sleep on the couch.

"Wh—what!" Butta stuttered, jumping to his feet af-ter seeing Toflon standing over him. He was looking cra-zy with his Mack 10 clutched in his hand.

"I said let's ride, nigga." Toflon swayed from side to side. Butta could see his friend wasn't in any condition to be out on a mission in his current state of mind. But he knew he was hurting, so he had to go easy with him.

"Listen, homie. You not acting like you're in your right state of mind looking for a nigga in these streets." Butta placed his hands on his shoulders, trying to steady him. His eyes focused for a minute, but he didn't recognize the person that stared back at him.

"Man, get your muthafuckin' hands off me," Toflon screamed, pushing Butta back on the couch with one hand startling Pookie who was sleep. "Nigga, I said let's ride. I mean let's fucking ride them bitch ass niggas that killed my fucking girl." Toflon stared down at Butta as if he didn't know him. Butta was in shock.

"A'ight, fam. You want to ride, let's ride," he replied, getting off the couch and grabbing his 9-millimeter and the keys to the van.

***

"Wow, Miss Jones. You look great," 40 said, checking out Vanessa's mom's hairdo.

"Don't she, Robert?" Vanessa said, agreeing with him.

Miss Jones pranced around in front of the mirror in his salon. She'd been out of rehab for three days now. Vanessa decided to treat her to a day of pampering. They went shopping, then to the spa. Now they'd just spent the last few hours getting their nails and hair done.

"You two sure know how to make me feel special," Miss Jones stated.

"Mom, you are special. Don't forget that." Vanessa then hugged her mother. "It's getting late, ma. Let me take you home," she said, grabbing her Prada bag out of her chair.

"Damn, baby. I thought you were going to stay with me tonight," 40 said, giving her his sad face.

"Oh, Robert. I forgot, but I got to take my mom home," she replied, giving 40 that same sad face back, hoping he would understand. Miss Jones watched the two lovebirds. She could see that her daughter really loved him.

"Vanessa, I can drive myself home. Go ahead and spend some time with your man. You've been with mommy all day. You know he wants some booty," Miss Jones said with a smile.

"Ma!" she shouted out, sending the whole shop into laughter. 40 stood there, shaking his head up and down in agreement with Miss Jones. "Mom, are you sure?" Vanessa inquired, unsure if that was a good idea since she'd just come home.

"Hell, yea. Now, give me the keys so I can get out of here," she said with her hand out, waiting for Vanessa to give them to her.

"Ok, mom. Let me walk you to the car." Vanessa and 40 walked her mother out to the Gold Lexus that was parked out front.

"I just love this car. I might have to ask my son if I can I have it," she said as she opened the car door, kissing her daughter good bye. "I'll call you once I get home, Nessa."

"Ok, ma."

"And it's was nice meeting you, Robert."

"It was my pleasure," he replied, holding Vanessa in his arms, as they watched her mother drive away.

***

"Damn, Toflon. We been riding for about two hours," Butta complained from the back seat. Pookie made a right, heading towards Jefferson. They were on their way to Fresh to Death Cuts.

"Yo, fam. Head over there to Blue Liquid," Toflon said with the Mack 10 lying across his lap. Ignoring Butta's whining ass, a gold Lexus shot by them that was headed in the opposite direction. Toflon and Butta shot up in their seats at the same time, trying to see if it was BJ's Lexus.

"Yo, Pookie. There go that nigga right there. Bust a U-turn," Tolfon told him, grabbing the Mack 10 off his lap. He had followed BJ a few times in the past, so he knew what he drove when he saw it. They followed the car for about six blocks until it stopped at a red light.

***

Miss Jones popped her fingers and danced in her seat while listening to the OJ's "Cry to Together" on the radio. She felt good being clean. Her son BJ was doing well as he had her living it up in Hampton. She didn't approve of his lifestyle, but she admired him for being a man. He'd stepped up and took care of her and her daughter. Miss Jones smiled again as she thought about her son as a van eased up next to her. She was jamming when she finally looked to her left. All she saw was a masked gunman, holding a machine gun.

Boom, boom, boom, boom, boom!

She heard the gun jumped in the masked gunman's hand, shattering glass into her face. Bullets flew, hitting her neck, chest, and arm. As a reflex, she stomped down on the gas pedal, sending the car into the intersection as it crashed into a parked car on the corner.

She could still hear the OJ's playing on the radio after the crash. She could also hear footsteps running towards her. She was thinking that help was on its way.

All I got to do is hold on, she thought to herself.

A figure appeared at the driver's side. She knew she was dead when she saw the masked gunman standing there with the machine gun in his hands. He looked confused for a second, but shrugged his shoulders, dropping 11 more bullets in her face sending her into darkness.

Chapter 20

Tashia sat on her couch waiting for BJ to show up. Things hadn't been the same ever since she overheard him confessing to Skalez' murder. Her mind was all over the place. She loved BJ with everything she had in her, but she didn't know if he would accept her after he learned about her past. If he rejected her, then she would make 40 aware of the situation. But if BJ embraced her with all her flaws, she would convince him to cancel the contract he placed on 40's life. She wasn't proud of the woman that she was, her mind drifting back to the night that Skalez killed Lance.

"Hey, Skalez," Tashia said through the phone before Skalez hung up.

"Yeah, what's good? Make it fast," Skalez replied.

"Let me speak to my dead boyfriend."

"He already listening," Skalez said, smiling.

When Lance heard Tashia's voice coming through the phone, he got sick on his stomach. He couldn't believe what he was hearing. His eyes got wide and his mouth dropped. "You dirty bitch. You been setting me up the whole time," Lance said, moving on the ground mad as shit handcuff wishing he could get his hands around Tashia's throat.

"I'll be that, but no hard feelings, baby. It was just business. You are a nice guy and all. I do hope that you find that one person you can spend the rest of your life with in another life," Tashia said coldly.

"I'ma kill your ass when I see you," Lance stated with pure hate in his voice.

"Nigga, you already dead. Catch me in hell, motherfucker. And you better have your fire boots on. I still

might be burning your money when I get there, you little dick bastard," Tashia said, laughing.

BJ's keys jiggled in the lock of the front door, bringing Tashia out of her past and back into the future. When he saw her sitting on the couch looking all good in her designer sweat suit, he smiled and licked his lips. He was deeply in love with this woman.

She wiped the tears from her eyes, trying not to let him catch her crying, but it was too late. He walked over to her and took a seat next to her, placing her hand in his.

"Hey, baby. What's the matter? Why you sitting here crying?" BJ asked, searching her face for a answer. She remained silent for a minute, but to him it felt like forever. She wiped her nose with the sleeve of her sweat suit.

"BJ, I love you," she began.

"I love you back, so what's the problem?" he asked with concern. Tashia let out a sigh. She figured it was now or never.

"Remember there was something about my past I needed to tell you about?"

"Yeah."

"Well, you need to know before we go any farther in our relationship that I used to be a grimy bitch. I used to set niggas up for money. I used to set niggas up for a nigga named Skalez." Tashia made eye contact with BJ for the first time. His neck and back broke out in goose bumps, but he played it cool.

"Okay," he replied, encouraging Tashia to go on.

"And I know you were the driver for 40 on one of the capers we pulled," she said, still gripping his hand. He was speechless, searching her eyes for betrayal, but he didn't see any. *How did this Skalez shit come back to me like a full circle,* him thought to himself.

"How you figure some shit like that?" BJ asked, trying to figure out how much she knew.

"Lets keep it real, BJ. I know you killed Skalez."

BJ snatched his hand away from her and stood up. "You don't know shit!" he yelled.

"I do. I heard you tell Homicide Jack you did it. I know that you put a ticket on 40's head!" Tashia shot she back.

He stood there puzzled, then it hit him like a ton of bricks. *She must have heard me talking to Homicide Jack,* he thought to himself. "So, what are you saying, Tashia? You going against me?" he asked.

"All I'm saying is I accept you and your flaws. Please accept mines. I'll protect your secrets if you protect mine. I'm in love with you, BJ. All I want is for you to love me the way that I love you." Tashia got up and walked over to him, meeting him face to face. "This doesn't have to break us apart. It can actually unite us and make us stronger."

She hugged him for dear life. Right then, he knew he had to make a choice: either kill her or make her a permanently number one in his life.

He backed away from her, staring in her eyes and getting down on one knee.

"Tashia, I accept you as you are, flaws and all, but I have a question to ask you." BJ paused, gathering his thoughts. "Will you marry me?" he asked, pulling out the black box he purchased from Aymir's Jewelers. Opening the box, he exposed the platinum 2-karat diamond ring. Tashia covered her mouth shock, crying tears of love. Her voice quivered as she spoke.

"Ye—Yes, ba—baby. I'll marry you!" Tashia's hand trembled from great anxiety as he placed the ring on her ring finger. He smiled, standing to his feet. He cuffed her face in his hands and placed a passionate kiss on her lips. Their tongues danced in each other mouth. She pulled him closer to her, sticking her tongue farther down his throat before pulled away from her.

JIBRIL WILLIAMS

"Tashia, I don't care what you've done in your past. All that matters to me is we never part and that we become one in any and every thing that we do. I make this oath not only to be your husband, but to be you partner and your friend. Can you say the same?" BJ asked with sincerity.

Tashia nodded her head up and down in agreement. "Yes, BJ. I can."

They embraced, holding each other until their hearts became one. His phone rang in his front pocket. He let it go to voicemail at first, but the caller called back, so he answered.

"Hello."

"Bryant, this is Vanessa. They shot, mommy. They killed ma, Bryant!"

"What! Nessa, where are you?"

"I'm at the hospital," she spoke through tears. BJ hung the phone up and told his soon to be wife, "Someone just killed your mother-in-law."

He walked out the door with murder on his mind.

Chapter 21
7 Days Later

BJ still couldn't wrap his mind around why anyone would want his mother dead except for mistaken identity since she was in his car. He couldn't think of too many known enemies he had, but. whoever it was had committed a grave sin in his book.

BJ could only think of two individuals that could be responsible. That was 40 or Toflon after the confrontation they had at the club the night of his birthday. The death of his mother even had him looking at Homicide Jack differently. He knew if 40 had something to do with it, Homicide Jack was the only one that knew that he wanted 40 dead.

At times, he looked at her as if she could have been the person behind his mother death, but the way she cared and comforted him in his time of distress took all the doubt away,

Burying his mother was one of the hardest things in life he had to ever do. He went to see his mother for the last time to say his good byes at the funeral home an hour before the funeral started before anyone got there. Once everyone had walked away from the burial site, he walked up to his mother's grave and dropped a few dozen roses on her casket.

No one had seen BJ in a week except Tashia. She laid in the bed with him, bobbing her head up and down in between his legs.

She was trying to suck all the hurt he was feeling out of him. She took her tongue and swirled it around his bell pepper shaped head, while she massaged his balls. BJ placed his hand on the back of her head, encouraging her to go down farther on his dick and moaned, "Mmmmmm."

Tashia placed him fully in her mouth, making his manhood touch the back of her throat while wetting his manhood down with her saliva. She then pulled him out her mouth, puckering her lips as if she was going to kiss the dick. She softly patted his solid eight inches against her lips. For some reason, this technique made BJ's manhood swell to the max. She pulled him back in her mouth and continued to give him the best he had in his life.

"Shit, baby," BJ whispered through clenched teeth. His toes cracked and popped. She could feel BJ releasing in her mouth. He locked his ass cheeks and arched his back off the bed, spilling his seed in her warm wet mouth. "Arrgghhhhhhh!" he roared out.

Tashia didn't stop. She sucked and milked him until he was limped and empty. He lay on his back, breathing hard. Tashia swallowed, then reached over him to grab the Atimo stuffed with Kush off the nightstand next to the bed. She lit it and took a few pulls of it before she passed it to BJ.

"You cool, baby?" she asked him while he hit the Atimo.

"I'm cool as a fan. No sweat," was the only reply he gave her.

Since the death of his mother, he became cold and distant. Not towards her but in his all around dealings. She knew that sometimes that happened when you were living the street life. It's something BJ mostly learned to live with.

"I'm going to take a quick shower, then I'm going to order us something to eat," she said, getting out of bed.

"Sounds good to me," he replied, watching her naked ass clap together as she walked to the bathroom.

***

"Yo, 40. Grab some blunts while you up there," Wallo yelled from the back of the gas station store.

"I bet you would tell a nigga to get the blunts with your broke ass," 40 shouted back, making the young female behind the counter laugh.

"Nigga, ain't nothing broke about me. I just don't like spending mines unless I got to, nigga. That's how you get ahead in this game, by saving and not spending," Wallo told him, grabbing a bag of Lays chips off the chips rack.

40 and Wallo had become close over the past few months. Their relationship wasn't like him, Skalez and Block, but they were getting there. The store bell alerted the clerk and 40 someone had just entered the store.

40 placed his eyes on the old timer. He had the aura of a man who had been in the streets back in his day. He had swagger about himself. 40 never saw the man before, so he headed to the beer cooler to select a beer for him and Wallo.

"Yes, may I help you?" the clerk asked as the man approached the counter.

"Yeah, give me a pack of Newport one hundreds and five of them Jackpot scratch tickets."

The clerk rang the man's items up. "That will be ten dollars and eight five cents, ,sir," the clerk said with a smile. The older man paid, putting the Newport cigarettes and scratch tickets in his front pocket before he exited the store. The clerk stared with lust in her eyes at 40. She was hoping he noticed then give her his number or at least ask for hers.

He grabbed 2 six packs of Miller Genuine Draft. "Damn, Wallo. What the fuck taking you so long? I know your broke ass not back there stealing these people's shit," 40 said, laughing.

"He better not be back there stealing," the clerk said, falling in with 40.

"Man, what you two talking about? I got enough bread to buy everything in this bitch," Wallo shot back, holding up two big wads of money in the air.

"Well, hurry the fuck then. We got—" The door bell chimed, cutting 40 off mid sentence once he saw the person was wearing a rubber clown mask, clutching a Tech 9. 40 went into slow motion, dropping the beer as he went for his P89 Ruger. "Wallo, it's a hit!" he yelled, falling to the floor before he sent 4 shots through the Little Debbie cake rack.

Boom, boom, boom, boom!

Cakes and cream-filling went everywhere. Wallo ducked down in the back of the store. He gripped his 45, took one deep breath and stood up, and firing.

Boom, boom, boom, boom!

He fired shot, grazing the masked gunman across his chest, and sending him stumbling back. The gunman trained the deadly weapon Wallo's way and open fired, sending Wallo for cover.

Pop, pop, pop, pop, pop!

The clerk was screaming at the top of her lungs every time a shot rung out. 40 shot some more through the Little Debbie rack. *Boom, boom, boom, boom!*

He was trying to get a better shot, but now the gunman was spraying the whole store, keeping him and Wallo pent down. Glass and derbies was flying everywhere. Wallo changed positions, trying to get a shot. He could tell the masked gunman was experienced. The clerk was silence in mid-scream.

40 knew the gunman should be running out of bullets soon. That meant he was either going to reload or make run for it. Either way, 40 was going to wait for the opportunity.

Just as he thought, the gunman stared back at him as he peddled out of the store, still banging shots at him and Wallo.. *Pop, pop, pop, pop!*

Once the gunman made it outside, he turned and sprinted off. 40 jumped up off of the floor and gave chase to the parking lot out where the gunman had jumped into a beat up hooptie. He sent five shots his way.

Boom, boom, boom, boom!

The hooptie tore off out of the gas station. Then he ran back in to check on Wallo. "Wallo!" he called out.

"I'm in the back trying to find the tape!" he shouted back.

"Hurry the fuck up. The police will be here any minute," 40 yelled.

He thought about the clerk that worked at the store. He knew he couldn't leave any witnesses. He walked behind the counter where he found the clerk lying in a puddle of blood. She had a hole in he chest, gasping for air.

"Hel—help me." The clerk fought to breath. 40 slightly shook his head. He lifted his gun and put one in her head.

Wallo walked up behind him, startling him. "I got the tape. Lets go." Wallo hit the cash register, taking all the money out of it. Then they both made their exit out the gas station.

JIBRIL WILLIAMS

Chapter 22

"Fuck! Fuck! Fuck!" LJ yelled, beating on the steering wheel of the hooptie before he snatched his mask off. He couldn't believe he missed. Old age must have caught up with him, throwing off his aim. He made a left on Martin Luther King Drive, pulling into an alley in the middle of the block. He then drove the to the end of the alley, parked and got out. He wiped everything down with an old T-shirt he had laying in the back seat, making sure he was removed any of his fingerprints.

He then went to the trunk of the car and opened it. He broke the Tech 9 down and placed it inside of an empty Timberland box. He worked fast as he grabbed the bundle of newspapers off the floor of the truck, spreading them across the inside of the hooptie. He got the gas tank and opened it, tightly twisting and pushing the newspaper inside of it. .

He then lit the newspaper in the hooptie, then the paper hanging out of the gas tank before jogging off. Once he was out of the alley, he waved down a cab at the end of the block. As soon as they drove off, he heard a loud explosion alerting him the car had exploded.

He laid his head back on the headrest, fishing his phone out of his pocket. The Timberland box rested next to him.

"Hello," a voice answered on the third ring.

"Homicide Jack, this is LJ. I missed."

He sighed. "LJ, you taking too long, my man."

"Naw, I'm just having a bad night."

"Man, get the fuck on it and stop playing with that nigga. You want this bread or not?" he shot back angrily.

There was a long pause on the phone. LJ didn't like how Homicide Jack was addressing him, but he swallowed his pride.

"Yeah, I want that bread. I'm on it," he stated, disconnecting the call.

***

Toflon, Pookie and Butta had been lying low since the shooting. They learned through the new the person that was driving the Lexus was BJ's mother. Pookie was feeling fucked up about the situation, but he didn't dare express how he felt. He wasn't down with killing no one's mother. He was in the game to get some quick money the fast way, the ski mask way. But Toflon and Butta could care less about killing someone's mother.

"Yo, fam. Pass the weed, nigga. You over there babysitting the blunt," Butta said to Toflon.

"Nigga, this my muthafuckin' weed. I bought this shit here!"

"But who bought the damn blunts?" Butta shot back. Pookie just sat on there on the couch shaking his head at his two partners in crime.

"Man, I'm not trying to hear that shit!" Toflon replied, hitting the blunt and passing it to Butta.

"What are we going to do about the nigga BJ?" Butta asked, taking the blunt from him..

"Nigga, it's on and popping. We gone get back on that nigga tonight. It's time we snatch this nigga," Toflon answered, getting hype.

"It's about time. A nigga's pockets is running low," Pookie said, sitting on the couch.

"This is the best time to catch this nigga slipping. He vulnerable right now dealing with the loss of his mother," Toflon told them both, rubbing his hands together.

Chapter 23

Vanessa was trying so hard to hold herself together after loosing her mother. It hurt her so bad, especially after seeing her clean off of drugs and full of life. She knew BJ was taking it the hardest, not seeing or hearing from him in days. The only reason she knew he was alright was because of Tashia who kept her updated.

Vanessa checked her phone to see if 40 had called her. He didn't come home last night, so she was beginning to worry about him. She threw her phone on the bed. "Where are you, baby?" she whispered to herself, getting out of the bed and walking in the kitchen to get some juice. The house phone startled her while she held the refrigerator door open. "Oh, shit!" she said, holding her chest. She grabbed the cordless phone off the counter. "Hello!"

"Hey, sis," she heard when she picked up.

"Bryant!" Vanessa got excited finally hearing her brother's voice.

"Yeah, sis. It's me," BJ said, turning on the their block.

"Where the hell you been? I need you." Vanessa was upset with her brother for abandoning her after their mother's death.

"I just turned on our street. Meet me at the car," he told her before he disconnected the call, ignoring her question.

She ran into the bedroom and threw on some sweat pants and house shoes, going outside to meet her brother. BJ's Charger pulled up, looking cleaner than any mutha-fucka sitting on big rims. Vanessa loved his car. He stepped out his car and embraced his sister.

"I'm sorry, Nessa. I just couldn't be there tor you in that capacity," BJ whispered in his sister's ear while they embraced.

"But you could have at least called me, Bryant. I was worried about you like crazy." Vanessa held on tightly to her little brother.

"I know and I'm sorry, sis." BJ kissed his sister on the cheek.

"How you been holding up?" he asked, breaking his sister's embrace and looking into her eyes.

"I'm better now that I got my brother back," she replied, looking into his eyes. The little BJ she used to know was gone and the person she was now looking was cold.

"I came by here to drop some money off." BJ walked to the trunk of the Charger and opened it. He grabbed a duffle bag and handed it to her. "I need you to put this money in the safe for me."

"Alright, but you do know I don't have the combination, right? And I hope you don't think you're leaving anytime soon. You will at least allow me to cook you some breakfast," she said with her hands on her hips.

BJ knew his sister wasn't going to let him out of her sight no time soon. So he decided to stay for breakfast. "A'ight, Nessa. I'll stay for breakfast."

"Good, come on." She led the way into the house.

"Yo, I got to piss," he said once he entered the house. "Put the money up while I use the bathroom. I'll meet you in the kitchen."

"Okay, but give me the combo to the safe."

"It's fourteen, sixteen, thirty-two," he told her, headed to the bathroom.

Vanessa walked into his room, going to his walk-in closet. The safe was located in the back of the closet. She pushed some clothes to the side that concealed the safe. She turned the dial to the combination he had given her.

Once she matched the last number, the lock popped and the door swung open. Her eyes jumped out her head.

"Damn, my little brother is doing it big," she said to herself, looking at all the money that was stacked nice and neat inside. She began to empty the duffle bag, stacking the money with the rest that was already in the safe. Before she closed the safe, something caught eye. "What's this?" she asked to herself.

She grabbed the purple Royal Crown pouch and opened it. A chain fell out. She turned the chain over in her hand. The diamond crusted Jesus piece felt heavy in her hand.

"Damn, I like this," she said, turning the chain over in her hand examining the full beauty of the jewelry. *I've never seen my brother wear this*, Vanessa thought to herself. She placed the chain back into the pouch, closing the safe. She made her way back to the kitchen, where she caught BJ drinking orange juice straight out the container.

"I know your ass not in here drinking out the container," Vanessa scolded him.

"Oops, my bad, sis. A nigga was thirstier then a stripper working at Blue Liquid." BJ screwed the top back on the carton and placed it back in the refrigerator.

"BJ, you better get that orange juice out that fridge. Don't nobody want to drink that stuff with all that backwash you just left in that OJ. I don't know where your mouth been at," she teased.

"Oh, your chicken noddle soup head ass got jokes, huh?" BJ shot back, smiling.

"Boy, you got nerve talking about somebody's head. You know damn well you got a milk jug head." Vanessa smiled back at her brother. BJ looked at her and saw his mother in her.

"You know you got ma smile, right?" he asked as Vanessa eyes became sad.

111

"I know. I miss her so much, BJ. I can't believe she's gone."

Vanessa's eyes began to tear up. She walked past BJ and got the eggs out the refrigerator, placing them on the counter.

"I miss her too, Nessa. It's my fault that she's not here."

"BJ, don't say that shit!," Vanessa shouted, turning to face him.

"No, Nessa. She was driving my car. Whoever killed her thought it was me behind that wheel of the Lexus."

"So, it's my fault too, then because I gave her the car to drive," Vanessa replied.

BJ didn't think of it like that. The last thing he wanted was his sister carrying the blame of their mother's death on her shoulders.

"Don't feel like, Nessa. Just know when I find out who did this, I'm killing his ass."

"Look, BJ. I don't want to talk about that right now. All I want to do is enjoy my brother's company. So, how do you want your eggs?"

"Scrambled with cheese," he told her, pulling a seat up at the kitchen table.

"So, what's up with that chain you got stashed in the safe?"

"Oh, nothing."

"Since there's nothing up with it, then can I have it?"

"Hell nah!"

"Damn, bruh. Why you say it like that?"

BJ let out a sigh. "It's not my chain, Vanessa."

"Well, whose chain is it then and why you got it?" she asked.

"You remember my man, Lil Chris?"

"Yeah, I could never forget his little dirty ass," she said, cracking four eggs and placing them in the bowel.

"Hold up. Didn't he get killed or something like that in a home invasion?"

"Yeah, well the chain belongs to him. That's all I have to remind me of him. To me though, the chain reminds me that what goes around comes around."

"What you mean 'what goes around comes around'? That sounds like a book title or something," she said with her face balled up.

"Sis, I can't go into much details, but that chain has history. Niggas been dying about that chain," BJ said, standing up and taking the pancake mix out the refrigerator. Lil Chris' brother Peanut was the original owner of the chain before he got killed. Then the person that killed Peanut, got killed once he was found wearing the same chain. That same person was also responsible for killing Lil Chris' brother Peanut. BJ looked at his sister to see if she was following him. "Lil Chris knocked off the nigga who killed his brother after he handled his business."

"So, were you with him when he was handling his business?" Vanessa searched her brother's eyes to see if he would lie to her.

"Naw, sis. I wasn't," BJ replied, turning his head away from her. Vanessa knew he was lying, but she let it go for now.

"So, how you end up with the chain?" she asked, beating the eggs in the bowel. BJ turned his head away from his sister again, another dead give away that he was being untruthful. "He told you to hold it the night he got killed?" she quizzed him. "So you weren't with him the night he got killed?"

"Damn, Nessa. You acting like the fucking police with all these cross-examine questions you're asking," he barked at his sister.

"Naw, boy. We're just having a conversation," she said, rolling her eyes and neck at his sudden attitude.

"My bad, Nessa. Let's just talk about something else and have a good breakfast."

"Yeah, lets do that, little bruh," she said, pouring the eggs into the skillet.

Chapter 24

40 couldn't put a finger on who was out to kill him. Last night had him on high alert. The way that nigga came into the store spitting that Tech 9 made him realize two things. One, the nigga behind the clown mask came with a purpose and two, if he ever found out who was the shooter, he couldn't play any games with him at all.

40 felt if Wallo wasn't there, the shooter probably would have succeeded at killing him. He couldn't help but wonder if the shooter was the same person that killed Block and Skalez. He had to apply more pressure to the streets and find out who killed his friends.

He turned on Vanessa's block, slowing down when saw a money green Charger with big rims on it, backing out of her driveway. "What the fuck?" he said to himself. He couldn't tell who was driving, but he knew it was a dude behind the wheel. 40 let his 745 series coast until the Charger turned off the street.

He whipped his B.M.W into the driveway where the Charger was just parked and got out. He scanned his surroundings, patting his hip where his P89 Ruger rested. He walked to the door and knocked. Moments later, Vanessa came to the door.

"Robert!" she shouted and jumped into his arms, wrapping her legs around his waist. "Baby, what happened to you last night? You didn't return none of my calls," she asked him.

"Shit kinda got outta control last night. Something came up that needed my under divided attention."

"But at least you could have called me for a minute to let me know that you were okay or to put me to bed," she whined.

"My bad, Nessa. I just got caught up," he said, kissing her on the forehead.

JIBRIL WILLIAMS

"Well, are you hungry? I made some breakfast for me and my brother, Bryant. He just left."

"Was that him in the green Charger?" 40 asked.

"Yeah, that was him." Vanessa climbed out of her man's arms with her sweat pants all in the crack of her ass. She walked to the kitchen with his eyes glued to her ass. He could tell she didn't have any panties on by the way her ass cheeks jumped and banged together in her sweat pants. "I wish you could have met him," she said, while grabbing a plate out of the cabinet over the sink.

"I will meet him, baby." 40 walked behind her, kissing her on the neck. He snatched her sweat pants down all the way down to her ankles in one swift motion. Vanessa grabbed a hold of the edge of the sink, pushing back on his hardness while arching her back. 40 placed his 9-millimeter on the counter next to the sink, releasing his throbbing member. He entered her without hesitation, slamming into her as he sent her to the balls of her feet. He quickly caught a rhythm, sending his pelvis into her juicy ass.

Wack, wack, wack, 40's pelvis sounded off as it made contact.

"Oh yeah, Robert," Vanessa cried out, moaning. "Yessssss! Robert!" she screamed, matching his rhythm. Vanessa felt his manhood swelling inside of her. She knew it wouldn't be long before he released his load.

He palmed Vanessa's cheeks, spreading them wide. Then he inserted his right thumb into her asshole. Even though she'd never been penetrated there before, it made it easier for her to nut.

"Oh shit, baby. I'm cumming. I'm cumming, baby," Vanessa sounded off, causing him to look down at his hammer slamming in and out of her. He could see how thick her juices coated his dick. The sight drove him over the top.

40 gave her a few more hard thrushes, locking himself in with his ass cheeks tightly clenched as he released his load inside of her. Vanessa worked her love box in a small circular motion, getting every drop out of him. They both pulled their pants up and shared a long intimate kiss. Their fuck session was well overdue.

"Damn, Robert. You must be really missing me. You haven't been in the house 10 minutes and already got the dick in me," she said, giggling.

"You know I can't be around you too long without stirring up that good pudding you got," 40 stated, giving her that "I want to fuck you one more time" look.

"Is that right?"

"Yup!" 40 took a seat at the kitchen table.

"Well, would you like it if I told you I'm willing to let you stir in this pussy up all day, twenty-four seven if the offer for me to move it still stands?"

"Shit, baby. I'm ready. I been ready, but why the sudden change of heart?" he asked.

"Well, I told you when you first asked I couldn't because of my moms. But now she's gone and I'm pregnant."

"Pregnant?" 40 asked, jumping to his feet.

"Yeah, pregnant! I'm pregnant, Robert," she said, laughing.

"Yo, Nessa. Don't fuckin' play with me. Are you serious? Are you really carrying my seed in you?"

"Yes, I'm serious, Robert. Are you mad?" she asked now with concern in her voice.

"Hell naw, baby. I'm not mad. I'm happier then a muthafucka," 40 responded, smiling from ear to ear picking Vanessa up off the floor and kissing her as they started round two of sexing.

Chapter 25

BJ had been moving with cautious every since his mother had died. Homicide Jack tailed him everywhere he went. He even threw a few dollars at his connect and got him and his team bulletproof vests and mini 14s. He hired a group of young niggas just to sit across the street of both trap houses. If they saw anything suspicious they were to open fire and ask questions later.

BJ's money flow had pick up tremendously. Him and Bugg were doing some numbers. It seemed like the more money they made, the more Bugg got paranoid. But with BJ, the money he had the more he grinded. He had everyone with their ears to the streets about his mother's death. There was a $30,000 reward for any information that would lead to her killer.

He pulled at the trap house on 24th street. He hopped out his charger, he saluted the two young shooter sitting across the street and walk into the front door. Before he got to the door good, Homicide Jack was pulling up to the curb behind the Charger in his rental.

The trap house door opened with Moe-B standing behind it. He wore a mini 14 that was strapped across his chest. This was protocol at both of his spots. The workers must open the door all the times with their assault rifle strapped across their chests.

"Moe-B. What's up, fam," BJ greeted his top soldier.

"Man, ain't too much. Just getting this paper, as always. Man, I'm sorry about your moms," Moe-B said sincerely.

"Thanks, fam. You heard anything about that, though?"

"Naw, BJ. I haven't heard shit," he said, making eye contact.

"Where Lil Tate at?" BJ asked, scanning the living room.

Lil Tate wasn't in sight anywhere, ducking off in the bathroom on some shady shit.

***

"Man, we're going to put this shit together real soon," Lil Tate whispered into his cell phone.

"Nigga, when? I'm tired of waiting," Toflon told him, getting frustrated.

"Lil Tate, you shitty ass nigga. You been shitting all day. Bring your ass out here. BJ here!" Moe-B yelled from the other side of the door.

"A'ight, I'm on my way out!" he yelled, flushing the toilet.

"Toflon, I got to go. I'm going to get with you," he whispered again, ending the call.

***

"So, how is business?" BJ asked.

"Shit been going all right. The money coming in like crazy," Moe-B said, pouring his a drink from the Hennessey bottle.

"What's up, BJ!" Lil Tate said, coming from down the hall. He extended his hand, giving BJ some dap.

"You know me. I'm just trying to live." *Something seems odd about him*, BJ thought to himself. "You got that paper. I got to make moves."

Lil Tate reached in the liner of the back of the couch and removed two brown bags, handing them to BJ.

"How we looking on the work?" BJ asked, looking into the bags.

"We should be good until tomorrow afternoon," Lil Tate replied.

"A'ight, I'll send some work over tomorrow morning," he replied, giving Lil Tate and Moe-B some dap. BJ hit Homicide Jack on the phone.

"Yeah," Homicide Jack answered.

"I'm on my way out."

"Everything looks good. Come on with it," said Homicide Jack.

BJ walked out the trap house to find Homicide Jack and his young shooters spread out on the block with their burners posted against their legs. He hopped in the Charger and murked out. Homicide Jack got in his rental and followed.

***

Lil Tate sat on the couch in the trap house. Even though BJ and his Uncle had put him on, he envied BJ because he seemed to have it all. He hated that BJ was only 3 years older than him, but he was taking orders from a nigga like him. In his eyes, BJ was a sucka. Lil Tate felt he could run shit better than him. He really didn't really want to set him up, but the truth of the matter is he was terrified of Toflon and his crew. He had heard so much wild shit about Toflon, that he did it.

They ran into each other the other day when he was coming from the cornerstone buying blunts and condoms. He was nervous, running his mouth so much in Toflon's presence, he mentioned he was getting money with BJ on 24th street.

A light went off in Toflon's head, so he gave Lil Tate a choice. Either helped him rob BJ and get paid or die. Seeing Toflon's Mack 10 made it a no brainer for him, so he decided to help.

Chapter 26

40 walked into the salon feeling like a new man. After hearing the news Vanessa was having his baby, he felt for once he was doing something right. When he walked in the salon, he knew today was a blessed day for him. Mona, Skalez' mother, was sitting in a chair holding little Akeemah her granddaughter.

"Hey, 40!" Mona shouted as he walked in.

"What's good, Mona?" 40 said, hugging her. "And look at this pretty little angel right here." 40 pinched Ta'niyah's cheeks, making her laugh and kick her little legs.

"Thank you so much for buying this place and keeping my son's dream alive," Mona said, switching Akeemah from one hip to the other.

"Now, you know I wouldn't have it no other way. Your son was like a brother to me. I just couldn't see this place, his drams going down the drain."

"I know. That's why he loved you so much," Mona said, hugging 40 again.

"Oh, I got some good news, too," 40 said to her excitedly.

"What?"

"I'm going to be a daddy!" he shouted.

"Oh my God! Someone finally locked your crazy butt down, huh?"

"Yeah, Mona, and she's a cutie, too," 40 replied, laughing. " Oh, where's Paula?"

"She went to Popeye's to get us something to eat. She told me about y'all little fallout. The last time you two saw each other."

"Yeah? I wish that shit didn't go that way. All I wanted to know was the nigga name that killed Skalez killed." .Mona started looking around the shop as if she wanted to talk in private, 40 then led the way to his office.

"What's good, Mona?"

"I made Paula bring me here just for this reason." Mona bounced Akeemah up and down in her arms. "The police finally released the guy's name that Skalez killed in the home invasion."

"What's his name, Mona?"

"The detective said the guy was most likely not alone since the money that was missing out the safe. But he told me that during the robbery, Skalez must have gotten the jump on the robbers, pulling his gun and killing one of them while the other one killed him, then left with the money. The detective did tell me it was a juvenile. His name was Christin Young, but on the streets, he goes by the name of Lil Chris."

The name rung a bell in 40's head. "A'ight, Mona. I got it."

Mona looked at him and said, "Listen, 40. I didn't just give you this information so you can just sit on it."

"I'm not planning to," he spoke with sincerity in his voice.

"I want whoever is responsible for his death to have blood flowing. Then after that, get out these streets before the claim you like they did my son. You have a child to protect now."

40 understood everything she was saying. "Okay, Mona. Let me make some calls." Once she left the office, 40 jumped on his phone. It rang on the other end twice before someone picked up.

"Talk to me."

"Yo, Wallo. This 40. I got the nigga name that Skalez dropped the night he got killed."

"Who was it?"

"It's some kid named Christin Young. He went by the name Lil Chris."

40 gave all the info he received from Mona.

"A'ight, fam. I'm in the streets with this. Let me see what I can come up with, but keep this under your hat," Wallo said.

"Oh, I will," 40 said, hanging up the phone. He knew he was on to something now with the information he'd just gotten.

Chapter 27

Homicide Jack took another shot of Jack Daniels. The bar started to thin out. Watching over BJ had become a hectic job. Following his young boss all over Bad News seems to be more stressful than he could have imagined. The pay was crazy. He'd never made this type of money before in his life and he was indebted to him for believing in him.

He scanned the bar while lighting a Newport 100. He inhaled the nicotine deeply and blew it out through his nose. The barmaid made her way over to him. "Is there anything else that I could do for you, sir?" the barmaid asked

"Ummmm, yeah sure," he said real cool-like. "You could help me first by getting me another double Jack. Then you can tell me your name and why a woman like you that holds so much beauty is working in a place like this."

The barmaid quickly poured the double shot of Jack and set it in front o Homicide Jack. "My name is Channtel and I work here because it pays my bills," she replied with a slight smile on her face. "Now, what a fine man like you doing in here this time of night?" she asked with her own set of question.

"Ok, I can respect that, Ms. Channtel. A woman must make her paper," he said, drowning one of the shot glasses that she'd place in front of him. "And to answer the other part of your question, a brother in here because he's lonely and I have no one to go home to," Homicide Jack replied sincerely.

Channtel searched his eyes for any deceitfulness and found none. She encountered many slick-talkers while working at the bar, but for some reason, she didn't get that vibe from this man who confessed he was single and lonely.

"What's your name, handsome?" she inquired, showing her pearly whites in the dimly lit bar.

"Just call me Jack."

Channtel was the plain type, but under her black work slacks, she had an ass and hips with a set of B-cups that complimented them.

Her gray cat-like eyes enhanced her plain look. He looked at her, standing 5'5" and weighing about 145 pounds. She rocked a short bob that hung over the right side of her face.

"Nice to meet you, Jack," Channtel said, sticking her hand out to formerly greet him. What happened next was something straight off of TV as he took her hand in his, softly placing a kiss on it. Channtel blushed hard. She was one of the hopeless romantic types.

"It's a pleasure to met you," he spoke smoothly. For the next hour, they got to know each other. Their conversation came with ease and they found out they both served in the army. They exchange numbers, but kept talking with one another in between her serving customers. "So, are you going to let me take you to IHOP when you get off work?" Homicide Jack asked, not really wanting the night to end.

"Ummmm, I don't know. I got another hour in this place and right now my feet are killing me." A customer waved Channtel over. "Excuse me for a second, Jack. A customer is trying to get my attention." She walk over to the customer with a little extra in her walk because she knew his eyes would be on her. "Yes, may I help you?" she asked the customer once she reached him.

"Yeah, give the guy you're talking to another shot of whatever he's drinking and this, please." The guy handed Channtel a piece of paper and a ten-dollar bill, telling her to keep the change. She walked back over to where he was waiting. She didn't know how to feel about the note that was given to her for him. She just hoped no gay shit was going on.

"Well, you must be a real popular because that guy over there bought you another drink and told me to give you this," Channtel stated, giving him the note and filling up another shot glass of Jack Daniels.

He looked confused, looking back at the guy that sat in the corner of the bar. The guy placed his beer bottle in the air to acknowledge Homicide Jack's presence. He opened the note and it read, *You're looking for a mother killer.*

***

"Oh my God! I'm going to have a baby," Vanessa said to herself as she stood sideways in her bedroom mirror, poking her stomach out. She was three months pregnant, just fresh out of her first trimester. She rubbed both hands over her stomach. She could feel the life growing inside of her. " I hope that it's a girl so daddy and Uncle Bryant can spoil you crazy," Vanessa spoke to herself.

As soon as 40 got the new place ready, she was going baby shopping. He decided they were going to need a bigger place now they had a new addition to their household.

Vanessa was cool with that. She knew he would be a great father. She examined her breasts in the mirror. They seemed to be fuller and 40 enjoyed himself with them, too.

She stepped into a pair of black-laced panties with a matching bra. She came along way from that girl in the hood, well she thought she did anyway. She soon had to sit down and tell BJ she couldn't break the work down anymore with Tammy because she was pregnant, not wanting to put the baby in jeopardy. She wasn't sure how

129

BJ was going to act, but she had a good feeling he was going to support her.

Chapter 28

"Yo, fam. You better tell a nigga something," Toflon said, grilling Lil Tate.

"Man, okay. This what it is, you can't bum rush the trap house. There are always shooters sitting across the street from the spot. Plus, the doors are reinforced with a shooter, so the only way you're going to be able to get in the spot is through the bathroom window," he told him with a shaky voice.

"So, you want me and my men to crawl through a small ass bathroom window?" Toflon questioned with suspicion.

"Man, that's the only way unless you want to just shoot it out with the shooters. Then you still got to get through the reinforced doors and Moe-B with the assault rifle."

"Why the fuck you just can't let us in?" Butta asked, jumping in.

"Because my Uncle will know it was me that let you in." Lil Tate was hoping they would back off the caper.

"A'ight, it is what it is," Toflon replied, confirming he was moving on it. "So, when is the best time to do this, nigga?"

"In two days when BJ come through to grab the money and drop the work off," Lil Tate replied, wiping sweat from his face. "I'm going to go unlock the bathroom window, then I'm going to go play Madden with Moe-B. The TV will be up loud so he won't hear you coming through the window. Once everything is set, I will call you and let you know when to come in," Lil Tate had everything planned out.

"All right, in two days we get paid," Toflon said, giving dap to Butta, and then to Pookie, who hadn't said a word the entire time.

***

LJ watched 40 as he make his way into the Fresh To Death Cuts. He was trying not to miss this time. He was going to wait until the right moment to make his move. The last time he went at 40, it was on a humbug. He didn't even know he was in the gas station until he walked in to buy some cigarettes. He thought to himself when he saw him, *Hell, why not?* He then went to the car, grabbing the Tech 9 and a clown mask before he went in to getting it popping.

40 had been moving more cautious lately. LJ knew he would slip and he intended to be there to keep him down when he did with his 45.

Homicide Jack hadn't been making shit easy for him either. Every two hours, he was calling for an update. It was to the point now he wasn't even answering his phone anymore. He was now a constant distraction to him and his work. LJ knew one thing for sure and that was 40 had a bad bitch. He would love to fuck her. He palmed his crotch as his dick got hard thinking about 40's woman, Vanessa.

Chapter 29

Homicide Jack and Channtel had hit it off good. He loved how Channtel was off during the day. That gave him time to run the streets and handle shit with BJ, then at night he would hit her place of employment, waiting for her shift to end. Ever since the death of BJ's mother, he made it his business to be home no later than 12 midnight and that was cool with Homicide Jack.

Channtel rode Homicide Jack's dick smoother then a Mercedes's ride. She went up and down on him like a carousel. Her love juices trickled down his shaft on to his balls.

"Daddy, I feel it in my stomach," Channtel said, then moaned. "Why you always make love to me like you're never going to see me again, huh?" she asked, while biting down on her bottom lip.

Homicide Jack dug deeper into her. "Because I believe what goes around comes around and I don't never know when karma will be waiting for me around the corner. So, I stroke you like it's my last," he replied, palming one of her breast.

Channtel didn't ask any more questions. She just locked in on getting her nut. She loved how massive he felt inside of her. Homicide Jack began to thrust inside of her, causing his nuts to draw up, then spilling his seed inside of the condom. Channtel could feel his penis jerking inside her, which made her cum with him.

The both laid there in their after glow. Channtel sparked a cigarette up and took two drags of it, passing it to Homicide Jack. She got out of bed and went to the bathroom. He watched her ass bounce from side to side. *Damn, I'm caught up in the matrix.* Homicide Jack thought to himself. He never thought he would be laid up with a woman like Channtel.

For once in his life, he felt like he was on top. He had saved damn near every dime he made from working for BJ. He learned from past experiences that you saved everything and flossed later when you're out the game.

She came back into the room with a warm, soapy washcloth. She eased the condom off his now limp dick and washed his member clean. Then she dried him off with the towel she had around her neck. She then walked back out the bedroom. Homicide Jack thought to himself that he could get used to living life with a woman showing him affection that catered to his every need. He knew whatever he and BJ had going on didn't last forever either, so he had to start coming up with a exit plan.

"What are you thinking about?" Channtel asked, interrupted him thoughts..

"Nothing much," he replied.

"It's got to be something because you let the cigarette burn out," she said, pointing to the unlit cigarette in his hand. She took the cigarette from him and relit it.

"I was just thinking about life or should I say how to change my life," he told her, watching her relight the cigarette and taking a pull from it. She looked so damn beautiful.

"What type of life changes you are trying to make?" she asked, letting a cloud off smoke out her nose. That's another reason why Homicide Jack liked Channtel so much. She asked the right questions at the right time.

"You know, basically settling down, relocating and getting out the game.

"Well Jack, if that is what you want to do, then I'm behind you one hundred percent.." she stated, passing him the cigarette again. "But let me ask you. Am I included in these changes you're trying to make?"

Homicide Jack hit the cigarette one hard time and replied, ,"You could be."

She smiled, then eased down between his legs before tonguing and kissing his dick, bringing him back to a full erection.

Chapter 30

Vanessa wiggled into a black pair of jeans. She examined her thighs in the jeans. *Shit, I'm only 3 months pregnant and I'm already gaining weight,* Vanessa thought to herself. She then threw on a charcoal gray Michael Kors turtleneck. 40 planned on taking her out to dinner to celebrate the beginning of a new life in their lives. He also had plans to show her the new house he bought for her and the baby.

She so was excited to be going at with her man. She couldn't wait to see him and the new place that selected for them. Vanessa hit the power button on the remote and the video network *MTV* jumped on the 70-inch TV screen. Kayne West's video "Jesus Walks" was playing. Vanessa turned the volume up and began to rock with Kanye West. She was getting her groove on until she saw Kanye's Jesus piece swinging from his neck.

Her mind went to the chain her brother had in his safe. It was something about the chain that had its hooks in her. She constantly thought about that chain. She stood up popping her butt and snapping her fingers while making her way to BJ's safe. She turned the dial as if the safe was hers. On the last number, the locks popped and the safe door swung open.

Vanessa grabbed the Royal Crown pouch and dumped the chain in her hand. She couldn't get over how heavy the chain felt in hands. She placed the chain around her neck. She walked to the mirror to get a better sense of what she would look like with the chain on.

The chain stopped in the middle of her stomach. Once she saw how the lights in the room lit the chain up, she was sold on convincing her brother to let her it.

"Damn, this is me right here," Vanessa said to herself as she rubbed her fingers over the Jesus piece. "Shit,

Kanye's chain ain't got shit on mines." Vanessa then smiled at herself in the mirror.

***

Wallo walked into the shop and knocked on 40's office door. He hated coming there. It reminded him too much of his cousin Skalez.

"Come in," 40 yelled from the other side of the door. Wallo walked in, giving him a pound.

"What's good, Wallo," 40 asked, looking up from his computer screen.

"I just came through to give you some info about the nigga Christin Young." Wallo took a seat in the chair in front of 40's desk.

"What you got?"

"Well, come to find out, that the nigga Lil Chris used to hang on twenty-fourth street before he died. He was hanging tight with another young nigga name BJ, but this isn't the climax of the story. Word on the streets is BJ been doing real good for himself. He got two trap houses, one on twenty-fourth street," Wallo said with a sinister smile on his face.

"Oh shit! I know that nigga!" 40 said, jumping out his chair. "It all makes sense now."

"Let me know what you know," Wallo directed him, sitting on the edge of his seat.

"Remember I was telling you about the New York nigga Lance that me, Skalez and Block robbed?"

"Yeah."

"Well, the nigga BJ went on that caper with us that night. BJ must been mad about the cut we gave his fuck ass. He must be the one who killed Block and Skalez. BJ must have been with Lil Chris that night Skalez got robbed and murdered. With Lil Chris getting killed too, BJ must have took the money that came up missing. So that's the reason he got shit jumping on 24th street." 40 sat back in his chair, opened the bottom drawer and removed a bottle of Remy out, taking a drink straight from the bottle. "That bitch ass nigga even showed his face at Skalez' s funeral." 40 shook his head in disbelief.

"I say that we move on this nigga tonight," Wallo replied with murder on his heart.

"Naw, what we do is chill. We don't want him to know we are on him yet. That way, he won't see us coming. Plus, I got shit planned with baby moms tonight. We are celebrating our first child together," 40 told him, wiping spit out the corner of hi mouth.

"Okay, then that will give us some time to watch his trap houses and when it's the best time to move on him," Wall said, standing up to leave giving 40 another pound.

"We're finally going to get justice for you, Skalez," 40 said, hitting Wallo's fist.

JIBRIL WILLIAMS

Chapter 31

Butta and Pookie crept through the alley behind BJ's trap house on 24th street. "Man, where the fuck Toflon at?" Pookie asked Butta again.

"Man, I told you that he had another lick to pull off. Toflon trusts us to handle this shit right here ourselves."

"Fuck man, I feel better if all three of us was here," Pookie complained.

"Man, shut your crying ass up and come the fuck on," Butta said, getting tired of Pookie's complaining.

They reached the back of the trap house. Butta and Pookie looked around to make sure no one was watching them. They were dressed in all black, wearing ski masks. Butta reached the bathroom and just like Lil Tate said, it was unlocked.

"Give me a boast, nigga," Butta directed him, whispering. Pookie laced his hands together and Butta put his timber land boot in his palm of Pookie's laced hand. "On three. Now one, two, three." Pookie pushed Butta upwards the window by his boot. He caught hold of the ledge, pushing the window while Pookie held him in the air by his feet.

Getting through the window was a tight fit for Butta since he was on the chubby side. Once inside the bathroom, he stuck his arm out the window to pull Pookie through. Unlike Butta, he got in no problem.

They could hear the Madden game being played, someone just scored a touched down.

"You ready, young nigga?" Butta whispered to Pookie.

"Butta, I was born ready."

They both crept out the bathroom, Butta leading the way while Pookie brought up the rear. They tipped-toed down the dark hallway towards the living room. "A'ight, bitch ass niggas You know what time it is," Butta announced, walking out the hallway. What he saw made his stomach flip. Lil Tate was sitting in the middle of the living room naked and tied to a chair. BJ and Homicide Jack were sitting on the couch playing Madden.

"Drop the hammer," Pookie told them, putting the cold barrel of his gun behind Butta's ear.

"Man, what the fuck you doing?" Butta asked through clenched teeth.

"Drop the gun or I will drop you." Pookie cocked the 3S7 he held in his hand. Butta dropped his Glock on floor. BJ smiled at Butta, recognizing him as one of the dudes who tried to get in at the on club on his birthday.

"Where is Toflon?" BJ asked.

"For some reason backed out," Pookie said.

"So, he sent you and him to do a nigga's dirty work?" BJ asked.

"Man, fuck you!" Butta shouted. BJ pulled his gun out and pistol whipped the hell out of him.

"You bitch ass niggas killed my mother!" BJ brought the gun down, leaving a 5-inch gash in his head.

Homicide Jack and Pookie watched. Homicide Jack was cool, but Pookie's heart was racing. He didn't know if BJ was really going to give him the reward money for the info on who killed his mother.

He felt fucked up about Toflon killing BJ's mother. So once he heard on the streets that there was a reward of $30,000 for anyone who had information about his mother's murderer, Pookie followed Homicide Jack to a bar. When they got there, he put everything on the table, leading to an agreement with BJ where he would turn on Butta and Toflon.

Homicide Jack walked over and grab BJ's arm, stopping him from delivering another blow to Butta's head. Lil Tate was so frightened, he pissed all over himself.

"Let's stick to the plan, BJ!" he yelled, releasing BJ's arm.

He then walked over to the table and threw Pookie a brown paper bag.

Pookie looked inside and saw it was filled with small bills. Butta's phone started to vibrate.

"Good looking," Pookie said, stuffing the bag in his hoodie.

Homicide Jack pulled out his phone and punched in some numbers. The phone was answered on the first ring.

"Yo!" Moe-B said, answering the phone.

"Bring the van around," Homicide Jack told him, disconnecting the call.

He untied Lil Tate while BJ and Pookie snatched Butta up from off the floor. They heard a horn blow three times outside of the trap house. "A'ight, lets go," BJ ordered.

***

Toflon sat in the middle of the block watching BJ's trap house. He could feel something was wrong, so at the last minute, he opted out of the caper. He told Butta another move came up, but that him and Pookie should go along as planned. Toflon tried to call Butta, but he wasn't picking up the phone. BJ's young guns weren't even on post tonight.

Toflon had to get a closer look. He cocked his Mack 10 and got out the Ford 150. He threw the hoodie over his head, making his way up the block towards the trap house when a van came out the alley and parked in front of the house, blowing its horn.

***

Homicide Jack led the way with Lil Tate at gun point. The cold air of the night slapped his face. Pookie came out next with Butta in front of him, BJ came out last. Homicide Jack saw a hoodie figure across the street, but it was too late. The gunman raised a machine gun and opened fire.

Boom, boom, boom, boom, boom, boom!

Homicide Jack pulled Lil Tate in front of him, shielding himself from the wrath of the Mack 10 while returning fire.

Boom, boom, boom, his roared. Lil Tate caught three slugs in his chest.

BJ let off shots at the hooded gunman.

Bluk, bluk, bluk!

Butta tried to run, but Pookie hit him three times with the 357. *Boom, boom, boom,* lifting Butta's body up in the air. Pookie caught a slug to the leg and broke out, hopping around to the side of the trap house.

The Mack 10 kept spitting. *Boom, boom, boom, boom, boom, boom, boom,* finding its mark as Homicide Jack was hit in the thigh and shoulder before crashing to the ground.

Bluk, bluk, bluk, bluk! BJ kept shooting at the hooded gunman. The gunman sent more shots BJ's way.

Boom, boom, boom, boom, boom, boom, boom!

BJ caught two slugs to his chest, knocking the breath out of him. He dropped his gun and grabbed his chest. He never felt pain like that in his life. The hooded gunman stood over him, pointing his gun. Toflon pulled his hood from over his head, exposing his face. He smiles at BJ. "You killed Trici. They say what goes around comes around." BJ was gasping for air. Toflon pulled the trigger on the Mack 10. *Click, click.* But the gun was empty.

He heard screeching tires behind him. He saw the black van Moe-B was driving, hopping on the curb as it came towards him. Toflon took off in flight, the van

144

missing him by inches before it crashed into the side of the trap house.

Moe-B ran to his uncle, helping him into the van. He could still see BJ moving on the ground. He went and helped him up, feeling the vest he wore. He got him in the van beside his uncle.

"Yo, Moe-B. Make sure them niggas is dead and get the guns," his uncle told him. Moe-B gritted his teeth, going and grabbing BJ's gun off the ground. He ran over to Butta. He didn't see him breathing, but he shot him in the head anyway. He jogged over to Lil Tate and stared at him for a second. He hesitated knowing that Lil Tate was his cousin. He didn't want his blood on his hands until he heard his uncle's voice coming from the van.

"Do it!" Moe-B then popped his cousin in the melon, making his way back to the van before they burned rubber.

Chapter 32

40 exited the shops. He left one of his best employers there to close up for him, sliding behind the wheel of his B.M.W. He felt good about what he had learned from Wallo. "BJ, I'm coming for that ass, nigga," 40 said to himself as started the car, turning on the heat. He felt the winter night air biting, rubbing his hands over the heated vents to warm them up.

He put the car in gear and pulled away from the curb. He was on his way to pick Vanessa up. He had plans to take her to dinner and to the Mary J. Blige concert. Then from there, he was going to show her their new home where he planned to make love to her in every room.

40 pulled his phone out from his hip and called Tashia. It went straight to voice mail. He hung up and tried it again. This time, she picked up on the second ring. "What's up, Tashia. This 40."

"I know who this is. I saw your number on the caller I. D.," she said with much attitude.

"Damn, I detect someone is mad at me," 40 replied, turning the heat down.

"Hell yea, I'm mad at you. You don't know how to call a bitch!"

"Well a bitch don't know how to call a nigga either because I haven't seen you blow up my phone in a minute," he replied.

"Yeah, yeah. You got a bitch there," she said, while drying herself off with a towel after stepping out of the shower. Truth be told, she stopped calling him ever since BJ proposed to her.

"Okay then, but listen, I just found out the wildest shit ever! Remember the nigga that Skalez bodied the night he died?"

"Yeah," she replied,, her heart beginning to thump in her chest.

"Well anyway, the nigga was Lil Chris and he used to hang tight with a nigga name BJ."

Tashia hand shot to her mouth, mouthing the word "no".

"Come to find out, the nigga BJ was the one that went on that caper with us the night we grabbed Lance. So it makes sense, Tashia. That little nigga BJ must have killed Block and Skalez."

"Hold up!" Tashia interrupted. "Are you sure he did all that?"

"Tashia, I don't believe in coincidences. That nigga had something to do with killing my nigga," he replied, raising his voice.

"All I'm saying is don't be so quick jump the gun on this ,40," she urged him.

"If I didn't know any better, I would think you're try-ing to take up for that nigga," he stated, pushing down on the gas peddle, sending the car 10 miles over the speed limit.

"Come on, 40. Don't play me like that. You should know me better than that."

"I'm just saying, Tashia. We got this nigga and you second guessing me."

"I hear you, 40. I'm sorry for making you feel like that," she told him, slipping on a pair of thongs. "But look, I jut got out the shower. I'm standing here soaking wet. I'm going to call you back when I dry off and put some clothes on."

"Naw, look. I'm about to take my girl out. I'll call you in he morning," he replied, stopping at a red light.

"Okay. Be safe," she replied before ending the call.

***

WHEN THE STREETS CLAP BACK 2

LJ followed 40 three cars back. He thought 40 saw him when he picked up speed a few minutes earlier. He was waiting for the right time to make his move, driving with one hand on the wheel and the other on his 45.

***

Tashia called BJ's phone nonstop. He didn't pick up. She wanted to call his sister Vanessa so bad to ask if she had seen him. "Shit, baby. Come on and answer the phone," she said to herself, pacing back and forth across the bedroom floor.

***

40 blew the horn once he arrived in front of Vanessa's house. She came out looking flawless as usual wearing some black tight jeans and a Michael Kors shirt that matched her leather charcoal gray Michael Kors boots that stopped just above her calves. Her leather jacket was zipped all the way up to her neck, hiding her top underneath.

Vanessa got in the car with all smiles. "Hey, baby," she greeted him, planting a wet kiss on his lips with a little tongue.

"Hey, baby moms. You keep kissing me like that we won't make it to dinner," 40 said in between kisses.

She laughed. "Okay, let me stop. I'll just rest my hand right here until we get to going where we're going," Vanessa said placing her hand on his crotch.

He just shook his head, backing out the drive away and driving down the street. Ginuwine song, "So Anxious" came on the radio and Vanessa dance and sung from the passenger seat.

"Oh shit! That's my song," Vanessa said, snapping her fingers along with Ginuwine.

"It's nine o' clock, nine o'clock, home alone, home alone.
Paging you, paging you.
Wishing that you would come over my place, my place
After while, after while. Let me know, let me know.
We can't just keep talk about the last time
You was here, you were here
What we did... "

Vanessa seductively danced in her seat, eye fucking 40 as she sang along with the radio. 40 smiled and licked his lips. He couldn't wait to get her home to the new house, so he could dick her down good.

She was beginning to work up a sweat from her little performance. She could feel the sweat trickling down between her breasts. She unzipped her jacket and removed it all in one motion. 40 stop at the red light behind a red Dodge pick up.

The moonlight reflected off the chain Vanessa had around her neck, lighting the car up. When it caught his attention, his facial expression changed.

"What the fuck! Where the fuck you get that chain from?" 40 snapped, grabbing a hold of the chain around her neck.

"Just calm down, Robert. This is my brother's chain." Vanessa thought he was mad because she was rocking another nigga's jewelry as they stopped at the light.

"Bitch, this ain't your brother's chain! This shit belongs to my nigga Block! Who the fuck is your broth—." That was all he got out before gunfire erupted from a navy blue Caprice next to them, sending them both into darkness.

Boom, boom, boom, boom, boom, boom!

150

WHEN THE STREETS CLAP BACK 2
TO BE CONTINUED

JIBRIL WILLIAMS

ALSO, FROM LOCK DOWN PUBLICATIONS
TIL MY CASKET DROPS
BY CA$H

Chapter 1

Mayhem stood shirtless in the mirror checking out his well-defined body. His pecs bulged and his eight pack was testimony to a religious workout that he had maintained over the past two years while locked up in Fulton County Jail on a murder charge that was recently dropped.

He was tatted up like a mofo, sleeves and all. His body was a canvas that displayed his blood, sweat and tears. Amongst his many tattoos, three bullet wound scars on his stomach was encircled with a tat that defined him and it read: *Get It How You Live.* The red ink looked like blood against his blueberry black skin.

One of the tattoos on his right forearm paid homage to his creed: *90's Baby.* No other generation was like those young boys. They were turnt the fuck up and Mayhem was the worst and best of them, depending on which end of his gun a nigga found himself on.

He turned his head to the side and stared at his mother's name tatted on his neck. Underneath it was *RIP.* Mayhem was only twelve years old when she was beaten to death by her boyfriend but the pain in his heart was eternal, and the memory of that night was seared in his soul. Many believed that it was her murder that had turned him into a stone cold killah.

Tears welled up in his eyes and pain contracted in his heart as he recalled fond memories of her that he held onto with a death grip. A day at Six Flags over Georgia. A ride in a stretch limousine for his tenth birthday. Fresh Jordans and other gear, year round. Anything he wanted, she found a way to give it to him.

"You're my number one man," she had told him every day that he could remember.

"And you'll remain my number one girl," he said, now in a voice strained with years of hurt.

He fingered the platinum name tag with her name engraved on it that hung from a chain around his neck. Damn he missed her. He hated the bitch ass nigga that took her away from him with a passion. She had been a stripper and a prostitute but to him she'd been a Queen. His *All I need,* as youngins referred to their mothers in the 'A'.

"I'll see you soon, Mama," he whispered, biting down on his bottom lip. He grabbed his Glock .40 off of the dresser and tucked it in the waist of his black jeans.

He lived by the gun and expected to die by it too. Any day could be his last, and he was a'ight with that. As long as he went out letting his ratchet spit back he didn't give a fuck.

Mayhem slipped on a black t-shirt then he strapped on an Ultra Lightweight Kelvar bullet proof vest and covered it with a black hoodie. Lastly, he reached in the middle drawer of the dresser and grabbed his black ski mask and a roll of gray duct tape.

His baby mama, Dream, stood in the doorway of the bedroom watching him. "I guess you're going on a lick," she said with disapproval.

Mayhem didn't respond. Things weren't exactly gucci with them. He was only there because it was a place to lay his head and it allowed him to spend some time with his daughter.

There was a time when Dream was his boo, but that time had passed. While he was in county she was out there doing her. She had thought for sure he was going down the road and wouldn't see daylight for a very long time. Dream had let different niggas run up in her and hadn't put a dime on Mayhem's books since the second month after he'd gotten cased up.

Mayhem wasn't the type of nigga to try to regulate his shawdy's pussy from lock down but he had expected her to look out for him after all the shit he'd done for her.

When the murder charge was dropped two weeks ago and he was released, he went to live with Dream but he slept in the spare bedroom and he hadn't fucked her.

"So you're not going to say anything?" She asked, twisting her lips up.

Mayhem turned around slowly and gave her a hard glare. He paid no attention to the short lace teddy that caressed the curves of her luscious body and rested high up on her smooth brown thighs. "What do you want me to say, shawdy? I get it how I live. You know that."

"I know you're going to end up locked up again if you don't find something legit to do." She glared at him with those pretty light brown eyes that hid the disloyalty that resided in her heart.

"Humph," Mayhem chuckled. "What you want me to do, go work at Popeye's or some lame shit like that? I got a daughter to feed in there." He pointed towards the master bedroom where his baby girl, Brandi, was asleep in Dream's bed.

He lowered his arm and looked down from his 6'2" height at Dream who was a foot shorter. "And I didn't hear you complaining when I was hitting licks buying you jewels, designer shit, and that whip that's parked outside," he reminded her.

"Boy, boo," she replied, placing her hands on her hips. "I never asked for none of that shit so don't act like you robbed niggas to take care of me."

"You might not have asked for it but I don't remember you turning it down either," he countered. Keeping his voice low so that he wouldn't awaken his little princess.

"What are you trying to say, Marquis?" She knew that he didn't like to be called by his government name.

Mayhem peeped game. He smiled and moved her to the side as he headed for the door.

"If your ass end up back in jail don't call me because I'm not going to have no holla for you," she hurled.

"I know. That's your get-down. But you had some holla for a whole lot of other niggas that didn't give a fuck about you while I was cased up."

"Fuck you, bitch ass muthafucka!"

Mayhem stopped in his tracks. Steam rose off of his head as he slowly turned around and stepped back towards her with a scowl on his face. "Is that the way you talk to a G?" His tone was as hard as the steel in his waistband, and the vein on the side of his head pulsated like a bolt of electricity had shot through it.

Dream knew that Mayhem wasn't the type of dude to put his hands on a woman so she didn't cower. Instead, she went in harder. "You don't scare me muthafucka!" she spat, shoving him out of her space. "You think I give a fuck about you being a *killah!*" She drew out the last word with special emphasis. "Niggas in the streets might fear you but I don't," added Dream, getting all up in his face.

Mayhem licked his lips and swallowed the anger that bubbled in his chest. Had she been a dude talking reckless like that, he would've sent her ass home to Jesus.

"Lil' mama, when I walk out that door no matter what happens tonight I'm not coming back. You and me are done forever — straight up."

"I don't give a fuck. I hate your ass anyway," she screamed.

"You hate me? Why? Because I won't fuck your ratchet, disloyal ass? You made that bed shawdy now sleep in that bitch."

Dream swung at him but Mayhem easily blocked the blow. He shook his head at her pitifully. "You don't deserve a thorough nigga like me," he said with finality. Then he was out.

"Fuck you! Bitch ass nigga. That's why I fucked your boy, Bebo, while you was locked up."

Mayhem heard that slick shit but he let it bounce off of his back like water off of a duck's ass.

Sliding behind the wheel of his black 2012 Range Rover, he sighed heavily and blocked Dream and her bullshit out of his mind. She was just upset because he refused to dick her down.

Mayhem reached under the seat and pulled out a bottle of Hen Dog that he kept on deck. He popped the top and took a gulp straight to the head. "Ahhhh," he exclaimed with satisfaction as he felt its heat in his throat.

Pulling off, he turned on some Pac and let that real nigga shit get him in a zone.

Hell, 'til I reach hell, I ain't scared.
Mama checking in my bedroom, I ain't there.
I got a head with no screws in it, what can I do?
One life to live, but I got nothing to lose.
"Hail Mary!" uttered Mayhem.

WHEN THE STREETS CLAP BACK 2

Starting tonight he was taking no shorts and showing muthafuckas no mercy.

Chapter 2

Bebo was already parked outside of the *IHOP* on Roswell Road in Sandy Springs when Mayhem arrived. Mayhem parked next to Bebo's Lexus IS 250 and got out.

Bebo, a dark-skinned, tall, gangly dude with an egg-shaped head, unfolded himself out of his whip and greeted Mayhem with some dap and a chest bump. He smelled like he had just smoked a whole pound of weed.

"What it do, bruh?" he smiled and licked his chapped lips.

Dream's claim rung loud in Mayhem's head. *That's why I fucked your boy, Bebo, while you was locked up.* Even though his love for her was dead, he couldn't help looking at Bebo and wondering if it was true or not. But he tossed it aside and concentrated on the business.

"I'm ready to get these bands. What's up, is it still a go?" He asked, leaning on the hood of Bebo's whip.

"Yea," replied Bebo, lighting up a Newport and taking a pull.

Mayhem's brow furrowed when he noticed a Dread Head in the passenger seat. "Who in the fuck is homeboy?" he asked.

"Oh, that's my nigga, Jabari. He's gonna go up in the house with you."

"What?" Mayhem gritted. "I don't know that mutha-fucka." His mouth was a tight line.

"Bruh, he's official. Trust me," vouched Bebo.

"In God I trust. Everybody else gotta show and prove. Fuck you talking about?" Mayhem spat. "Nigga's always seem official until they get those ghetto bracelets slapped on their wrists, then all the ho come out of 'em."

"I hear you, dawg, but Jabari ain't that type of nigga. Ain't no ho in his blood. Plus, I need somebody with you when you go up in there because you're stupid with that bang-er. You can't kill the nigga you're going to jack, he's my wife's twin brother. She would lose her goddamn mind."

"Well, his ass better not buck or he'll lose *his* goddam mind — I'll splatter it up on the ceiling."

159

Bebo shook his head in exasperation. "See, you're wild as hell. That's why I'm sending Jabari in there with you to keep your young ass calm." He had heard vicious stories of how beastly Mayhem could be. It was rumored that one dude that the youngin had robbed for his chain had ended up in the trunk of his own car with three bullet holes in his head. Body—burned and charred.

Bebo shook his head at the thought of that happening to his wife's twin. He hurriedly waved his boy out of the car and made the introductions.

Mayhem acknowledged Jabari with a slight nod of his head, but he didn't lock fists with him. He didn't know that nigga.

Ten minutes later they were ready to ride out. Bebo looked at Mayhem and held his stare. "Youngin, this is a jack move not a murder. Demetrius is already drunk and y'all gon' have the drop on him so he's not gon' buck. Just get the birds and the money and come on out of there. I'll be parked down the street. Don't kill my brother in-law," he reemphasized.

"You don't have to keep telling me that. I heard you, fam," said Mayhem. He got in his whip and waited for Dread Head to get in.

Bebo put a hand around Jabari's shoulder and whispered, "Don't let that young nigga murk my people. If it come down to it, do what you gotta do."

Jabari nodded his head then walked around to the other side of the truck and slid into the passenger seat.

They drove off with Bebo behind them nervously puffing on his cigarette.

Under the cover of a dark summer sky Mayhem and Jabari moved quietly into Demetrius' backyard. They climbed the four steps that led up to the screened-in back porch and Jabari used a double-edged hunting knife to cut hole in the screen. With a gloved hand he reached in and unlatched the lock on the screen door.

Mayhem walked ahead of him, stepping over a child's bi-cycle that laid on the floor of the porch. He pressed his ear against the backdoor listening for the sound of movement but

160

all he heard was music. French Montana played in the background.

Nigga, I ain't worried 'bout nothin'
Ridin' 'round with that Nina
Ridin' 'round with that AK, that HK, that SK
That beam on the scope
Window down, blowin' smoke
Niggas frontin' be broke
Try rob me, gon' get smoked
That gun automatic, my car automatic
Ain't worried 'bout nothin'

The irony of the lyrics caused Mayhem to smirk under the black ski mask that covered his face. "Nigga ain't worried 'bout nothin'," he rapped along.

Jabari chuckled.

They slid their bangers out and got ready to do a kick door. Mayhem eyed a spot just under the doorknob. He raised his foot up and smashed the heel of his Timbs at the perfect spot.

The door frame splintered on the first kick and the second one sent the door crashing in. It slammed into the wall with a loud bang. With his Glock held high, ready to spit flames, Mayhem dashed into the den where the music came from. Jabari was right behind him with a pistol grip pump shotgun cocked and locked.

Bebo had said that his brother in-law wouldn't buck the jack but Mayhem was prepared in case he tried. He stepped into the dimly lit den, prepared to hit him in the melon with that heat. Beside him Jabari was locked in too.

They found Demetrius passed out on the couch with his mouth wide open. He was a large, overweight man that snored like a hog. His arms and legs hung off of the plaid couch and his big round stomach rose up and down with every bronchitic breath. Several empty Ciroc bottles and a half-smoked Swisher sat on the glass end table next to a bowl full of loud.

Mayhem stepped as light as a cat burglar. When he was in front of the couch he bent over, stuck his tool in Demetrius' mouth, and slapped him across the face with his free hand. "Wake your fat ass up," he growled.

Demetrius eyes slowly opened and he awakened to a nightmare. When he saw the masked robbers and felt the weight of that banger in his mouth, his eyes popped out of his head.

"How does the steel taste, fat boy?" Mayhem mocked.

Demetrius didn't respond.

"Oh, you hard, huh? You're a G — you ain't giving up shit?" Mayhem said with an overtone of derision.

"You got that right," he mumbled around a mouthful of danger. Mayhem removed the gun out of his mouth and cracked him across the head with it. "You think this is a game?" he snarled menacingly but Demetrius remained stoic.

With blood running down the side of his face he stared up into the threat of death and mocked it. "Fuck you! You might kill me but y'all ain't leaving here with nothin' but my blood on your clothes. If you was broke when you ran up in this bitch, you'll be broke when you leave out," he spat bravely.

His gangsta caught Mayhem by surprise — Bebo had promised that he would fold meekly — but it didn't deter the young beast from the mission at hand. He had gone up in there to get the nigga's trap and he wasn't leaving out without it. The only question was how much pain and torture Demetrius could endure before he broke.

"You might hold out for a minute but I'ma break your big ass," Mayhem said, leveling the Glock down at him. The gun clapped twice, echoing off of the walls. Demetrius' winced as hot pain sizzled in both of his shoulders and rendered his arms useless.

"How does that feel?" Mayhem taunted.

"Suck my dick."

"Oh, yea? A'ight, let's see which one of us will suck that muthafucka, you or me." He looked over his shoulder and commanded Jabari. "Duct tape his fat ass. I'ma teach him some respect."

Jabari set the shotgun down and stepped to the business. He slapped a strip of tape over Demetrius' mouth to muffle his cries, then he bounded his hands together behind his back and taped his ankles together.

Excruciating pain surged from Demetrius' wounded shoulders and throughout his entire body as blood soaked his shirt. Sweat beaded up on his forehead and ran down into his eyes.

Mayhem propped him up on the couch. "Suck your dick, huh?" he said again.

Demetrius just stared at him.

Mayhem stared back. *You'll blink before I do*, he said to himself.

He turned to Jabari. "Keep your tool on this nigga, and if he wiggle give him a new hairline," he instructed before leaving the den in search of the bathroom.

He returned a few minutes later with bounce in his step and a bottle of rubbing alcohol in his hand. A large lump formed in Demetrius' throat. He swallowed hard and tried to conjure up the courage to endure the imminent pain that was sure to come.

Mayhem stuck his banger in his waist and unscrewed the top off of the alcohol. Without uttering a word he poured some of the liquid in Demetrius' gunshot wounds.

Demetrius' screamed but it was stifled by the duct tape over his mouth. His large body rocked back and forth as the pain in his shoulders intensified. "You still hard, my nigga?" asked Mayhem. He poured more alcohol in Demetrius' wounds. Still the only reaction he got out of him were grunts and moans.

"Give me your knife," he said to Jabari. "And turn the music up."

His accomplice complied.

Mayhem put the sharp serrated edge of the blade against Demetrius' face and cut him from the eyebrow to the chin. His jagged skin laid wide open. "Now niggas can call you Scarface."

Blood mixed with sweat and ran down Demetrius's neck. He mumbled something that sounded like a submission.

"He's ready to talk." Jabari quickly cut in. He was relieved because Bebo had explicitly stated that they were not to kill him.

"You ready to tell me where that safe at, Big Boy?" Mayhem asked.

Demetrius nodded *yes*.

Mayhem ripped the tape off of his mouth. "Start talking."

Demetrius knew that his fate was already sealed; he could see that in Mayhem's cold eyes. He didn't fear death, he had resigned himself to that. What scared him was the torture that he was about to suffer. He looked up at Mayhem with contempt and hawked a glob of blood and spit at him.

Had he not been wearing a ski mask it would've struck Mayhem dead in the face. He smiled underneath the mask because he understood what Big Boy was trying to do. He was trying to make Mayhem murk him fast.

"It ain't gon' happen like that, fam. I'ma make you suffer," he taunted.

"Kill me man and get it over with," he pleaded on weak breath. Jabari was afraid that Mayhem was going to comply. He raised the pump and pointed it at the center of Mayhem's back. *If it comes down to it do what you gotta do.* Bebo's words replayed. Jabari gently wrapped his finger around the trigger. He didn't owe this lil' jit any loyalty. His allegiance was to Bebo.

"Where is the money and coke?" Mayhem asked Demetrius once more. He was running out of patience and he was about to turn up.

"Suck—my—dick."

Mayhem slapped the lamp off of the end table sending it crashing to the floor. The uneven light casted an eerie silhouette of him on the wall. He picked the knife up off of the table, grabbed Demetrius by the head and sliced off his ear, ignoring the shrill scream that escaped his mouth.

"Muthafucka wasn't listening no way," he spat as he slung the severed ear across the den.

Behind him Jabari was paralyzed by the brutality that he was witnessing. He wanted to blast a hole in Mayhem's back to stop him from murking Bebo's people, but he wanted the money and the drugs more.

He stepped forward and pleaded with Demetrius. "Tell him where the shit at and I promise you after we get it we'll be out. I'll call an ambulance to come and get you and take you to the hospital."

Demetrius was bleeding profusely and death had his name on its tongue. He was weak and fading in and out of consciousness, barely able to respond. But now that he saw his whole life flashing before him, he decided that he wasn't ready to go to that other side. He moved his head up and down indicating that he was ready to cooperate.

Mayhem put his ear close to Demetrius' mouth to hear his faint voice. When he divulged where the stash was at Mayhem caught a bigger rush from snuffing out that nigga's gangsta than he did from the come up he knew he would leave there with.

He sent Jabari to the stash while he remained in the den with Demetrius. After Jabari disappeared out of the door, Mayhem sat the knife on the table and yanked Demetrius's pants down around his ankles.

"I'ma teach you not to tell a G to suck your dick." He picked the knife up off of the table and touched the tip of the sharp blade to Demetrius' chest, drawing a trickle of blood.

Mayhem slowly slid the blade downward leaving a sticky red trail from Demetrius' chest to his navel and he was just getting started.

JIBRIL WILLIAMS

Chapter 3

Bebo had smoked a whole pack of Newports. He bounced his leg up and down and drummed his fingers on the steering wheel wishing he had another cigarette. Or a blunt! Anything to calm his frazzled nerves.

What the fuck was taking them so long? He wondered as his little beady eyes strained to see up the block.

He rubbed his onion head as every possibility of what could've gone wrong ran through his mind. He let out a sigh and his hands began to shake like a first-time thief.

Fuck these fools at?

Unable to take it any longer, he pulled out his cell phone and called Mayhem's number. When there was no answer he tried Jabari's phone and was relieved when he answered.

"Yo, what's going on in there? What's taking y'all so long? Is everything alright?" The questions came out in rapid fire.

"Bruh, this young boy is cray! He done cut your folks up real bad; slashed his face and sliced his ear off, and that ain't the half," Jabari reported.

"Fuck he do that for?"

'Cause Demetrius wouldn't tell us where the stash was at. I thought you said he wasn't going to resist? It had gotten real ugly up in here."

"Is D dead?"

"Not yet but he's losing blood like a mofo and ya boy Mayhem got that murking look in his eyes." Jabari's harried tone caused Bebo to damn near scream.

"Don't let him do that!" Bebo rested his head on the steering wheel and stifled back tears. That was not how it was supposed to go down. He regretted sending Mayhem's blood thirsty ass on this lick.

"What you want me to do, bruh? I'm in the safe now. You want me to grab the shit and leave Mayhem in this bitch face down?"

"Yea, smash that fuck nigga."

JIBRIL WILLIAMS

"A'ight, I'ma blow his whole back out. One." He disconnected and shoved his phone back down in his pants' pocket.

"How you plan on doing that?" The voice on the back of his neck was frigid.

Jabari's head snapped around. Now he too was looking into the eyes of an unmerciful killah.

"What's—up—fam?" he stuttered.

"I'm not your muthafuckin' *fam!*" Mayhem shoved his banger in Jabari's grill. "Bitches get their backs blown out. You calling me a bitch?"

"What you talking about?" He tried to play it off but Mayhem had been standing there listening to his end of the conversation.

"I ain't talkin' 'bout nun," he chuckled ominously.

Jabari glanced down at his shotgun; he had laid it on the floor to open up the wall safe. "Go for it. Maybe you're quicker than my trigger finger, we'll find out," Mayhem challenged.

Jabari's hands shot up and Mayhem's Glock popped off instantly. *Blocka! Blocka!*

Two quick successive shots disintegrated his head, sending brain matter, teeth, blood and flesh spraying everywhere. As his body fell back, Jabari reflexively grabbed ahold of Mayhem's collar and they crashed to the floor.

Lying on top of Jabari, getting his blood all over his clothes, Mayhem placed the gun point blank on his chest and squeezed the trigger three times. "No new friends," he spat.

Jabari's hands fell down to his sides and his bowels released.

Mayhem ignored the stench as he ran Jabari's pockets and fished out his cell phone. Checking the call log he confirmed what he already suspected.

Soaked in the nigga's blood, Mayhem stood up and finished emptying the safe. When he had everything inside duffel bag they had brought along he hurried back into the den.

Demetrius was already dead. Mayhem set the duffel bag down and walked over to the body. He yanked the knife out of dead man's chest and took ahold of his small flaccid penis.

168

Holding it at the base, he severed it away from the scrotum and stuffed it in Demetrius' mouth.

"Suck your own dick, fat ass nigga!" said Mayhem.

JIBRIL WILLIAMS

Chapter 4

Mayhem bent a few corners, turned off his headlights and parked a block behind where Bebo waited nervously. He eased out of his truck and crept up the street like a night stalker.

Bebo nearly jumped through the roof of his car when he heard a tap on the window. He turned his head to the left and saw a face whose image he would take to hell with him. His eyes bucked and he tried to slither down in the car seat to escape what he had coming to him. But there was nowhere to hide.

Mayhem didn't play no games with that nigga. He fired six shots through the driver's window finding his mark with five of them. Bebo's head and chest exploded in a burst of red, splattering all over the dashboard and the seats. Mayhem snatched the door open and got up close and personal.

He placed the gun in the center of Bebo's heart and sent his ass where all unofficial niggas belonged.

Back in the inner city of Atlanta, Mayhem pulled up at the New American Inn on Cleveland Avenue where he knew the desk clerk that worked night shift. He rented a room and hurried inside to count his loot and wash those niggas' blood off of him.

A half hour later and fresh out of the shower, he sat on the bed in his boxers staring at his come up. He had three birds and seventy bands. He blazed a blunt and reminisced on tonight's kills. Had he left behind any evidence that could tie him to the murder? He asked himself.

A slight stinging sensation on his neck caused him major concern. Jabari had scratched him when he grabbed ahold of him.

Damn, Mayhem fretted. He got up and examined the mark in the mirror; it was long and pretty deep. They would find his DNA under Jabari's fingernails for sure. "Fuck!"

When he looked closer Mayhem realized that his chain wasn't around his neck. Jabari had snatched it off as they crashed to the floor. The name plate with Mayhem's mother's name on it would seal his conviction.

Now the game plan had changed. Mayhem refused to wait around for those folks to come lock him back up. He had beaten the last murder rap, and he knew there was no way those crackers would let him escape justice a second time.

He grabbed his banger and posed in the mirror, flexing his pecs. With the other hand he touched the tat on his neck. "Mama, I'll make six carry me before I take a chance on twelve judging me," he vowed.

Available Now!

Stay Connected with Us!

Text **LOCKDOWN** to 22828 to stay up-to-date with new releases, sneak peaks, contests and more…

Thank you!

Submission Guideline.

Submit the first three chapters of your completed manuscript to ldpsubmissions@gmail.com, subject line: Your book's title. The manuscript must be in a .doc file and sent as an attachment. Document should be in Times New Roman, double spaced and in size 12 font. Also, provide your synopsis and full contact information. If sending multiple submissions, they must each be in a separate email.

Have a story but no way to send it electronically? You can still submit to LDP/Ca$h Presents. Send in the first three chapters, written or typed, of your completed manuscript to:

LDP: Submissions Dept
Po Box 870494
Mesquite, Tx 75187

DO NOT send original manuscript. Must be a duplicate.

Provide your synopsis and a cover letter containing your full contact information.

Thanks for considering LDP and Ca$h Presents.

WHEN THE STREETS CLAP BACK 2
Coming Soon from Lock Down Publications/Ca$h Presents

BOW DOWN TO MY GANGSTA

By **Ca$h**

TORN BETWEEN TWO

By **Coffee**

BLOOD STAINS OF A SHOTTA **III**

By **Jamaica**

WHEN THE STREETS CLAP BACK **II**

By **Jibril Williams**

STEADY MOBBIN

By **Marcellus Allen**

BLOOD OF A BOSS **V**

By **Askari**

WHEN A GOOD GIRL GOES BAD **II**

By **Adrienne**

THE HEART OF A GANGSTA **III**

By **Jerry Jackson**

LOYAL TO THE GAME **IV**

By **T.J. & Jelissa**

A DOPEBOY'S PRAYER **II**

By **Eddie "Wolf" Lee**

IF LOVING YOU IS WRONG… **III**

LOVE ME EVEN WHEN IT HURTS

By **Jelissa**

DAUGHTERS SAVAGE

By **Chris Green**

BLOODY COMMAS **III**

SKI MASK CARTEL II

JIBRIL WILLIAMS
By **T.J. Edwards**

TRAPHOUSE KING

By **Hood Rich**

BLAST FOR ME **II**

RAISED AS A GOON V

BRED BY THE SLUMS

By **Ghost**

A DISTINGUISHED THUG STOLE MY HEART **III**

By **Meesha**

ADDICTIED TO THE DRAMA **II**

By **Jamila Mathis**

LIPSTICK KILLAH II

By **Mimi**

THE BOSSMAN'S DAUGHTERS 4

WHAT BAD BITCHES DO

By **Aryanna**

<u>Available Now</u>

<u>RESTRAINING ORDER</u> **I & II**

By **CA$H & Coffee**

<u>LOVE KNOWS NO BOUNDARIES</u> **I II & III**

By **Coffee**

<u>RAISED AS A GOON I, II, III & IV</u>

By **Ghost**

<u>LAY IT DOWN</u> **I & II**

<u>LAST OF A DYING BREED</u>

<u>BLOOD STAINS OF A SHOTTA I & II</u>

By **Jamaica**

<u>LOYAL TO THE GAME</u>

176

WHEN THE STREETS CLAP BACK 2

LOYAL TO THE GAME II

LOYAL TO THE GAME III

By **TJ & Jelissa**

BLOODY COMMAS I & II

SKI MASK CARTEL

By **T.J. Edwards**

IF LOVING HIM IS WRONG…I & II

By **Jelissa**

WHEN THE STREETS CLAP BACK

By **Jibril Williams**

A DISTINGUISHED THUG STOLE MY HEART I & II

By **Meesha**

PUSH IT TO THE LIMIT

By **Bre' Hayes**

BLOOD OF A BOSS **I, II, III & IV**

By **Askari**

THE STREETS BLEED MURDER **I, II & III**

THE HEART OF A GANGSTA I & II

By **Jerry Jackson**

CUM FOR ME

CUM FOR ME 2

CUM FOR ME 3

An **LDP Erotica Collaboration**

BRIDE OF A HUSTLA **I & II**

THE FETTI GIRLS **I, II& III**

By **Destiny Skai**

WHEN A GOOD GIRL GOES BAD

By **Adrienne**

A GANGSTER'S REVENGE **I II III & IV**

JIBRIL WILLIAMS
THE BOSS MAN'S DAUGHTERS

THE BOSS MAN'S DAUGHTERS II

THE BOSSMAN'S DAUGHTERS III

A SAVAGE LOVE **I & II**

BAE BELONGS TO ME

A HUSTLER'S DECEIT I, II

By **Aryanna**

A KINGPIN'S AMBITON

A KINGPIN'S AMBITION **II**

I MURDER FOR THE DOUGH

By **Ambitious**

TRUE SAVAGE

TRUE SAVAGE II

TRUE SAVAGE **III**

By **Chris Green**

A DOPEBOY'S PRAYER

By **Eddie "Wolf" Lee**

THE KING CARTEL **I, II & III**

By **Frank Gresham**

THESE NIGGAS AIN'T LOYAL **I, II & III**

By **Nikki Tee**

GANGSTA SHYT **I II &III**

By **CATO**

THE ULTIMATE BETRAYAL

By **Phoenix**

BOSS'N UP **I , II & III**

By **Royal Nicole**

I LOVE YOU TO DEATH

By **Destiny J**

178

WHEN THE STREETS CLAP BACK 2

JIBRIL WILLIAMS

WHEN THE STREETS CLAP BACK 2
BOOKS BY LDP'S CEO, CA$H

TRUST IN NO MAN

TRUST IN NO MAN 2

TRUST IN NO MAN 3

BONDED BY BLOOD

SHORTY GOT A THUG

THUGS CRY

THUGS CRY 2

THUGS CRY 3

TRUST NO BITCH

TRUST NO BITCH 2

TRUST NO BITCH 3

TIL MY CASKET DROPS

RESTRAINING ORDER

RESTRAINING ORDER 2

IN LOVE WITH A CONVICT

Coming Soon

BONDED BY BLOOD 2

BOW DOWN TO MY GANGSTA

www.ingramcontent.com/pod-product-compliance
Lightning Source LLC
Chambersburg PA
CBHW070028260626
47159CB00005B/1981